Beneath The Thundering Sky

THUNDERING MOUNTAIN RANCH
BOOK ONE

NICOLE NEISWANGER

Calico
publications

For questions or and comments about the quality of this book, please contact us at calicopublicationsllc@gmail.com.

Publisher: Calico Publications, LLC

Cover Design: Covers and Cupcakes, LLC

Editor: Telltail Editing

Digital ISBN: 978-1-960600-08-0

Print Edition ISBN: 978-1-960600-09-7

For my sister, Sarah Fleming.
Thank you for your support, it means the world to me. While we may have been at odds as children, getting to know you as an adult has been an honor and a blessing in so many ways. I'm lucky to have such a beautiful sister.
I love you!

One

Pennsylvania
July 5, 1865

"One night with you is all I'm asking," Frannie said, her knuckles white from gripping the pale rose, velvet chair in the front parlor of her two-story clapboard house. Heat flared up her chest and sweat beaded across her forehead as soon as the question slipped past her lips.

"I can't believe you would even suggest that," Cole said, his face draining of color. He stumbled back, hitting the edge of the side table before he collapsed onto the rose and blue flowered chintz loveseat. His mouth opened and closed, but nothing more emerged.

If this wasn't such a serious matter, Frannie might've laughed at his shock.

He took big gulping breaths and looked at her as if she had asked the impossible, and she supposed she likely had. She was taking a big risk, but they had been friends since they were toddlers, and she hoped he would be open to her suggestion.

"Are you all right?" she asked, wanting to smooth away the frown from his lips.

He paused, shook his head, and sighed. "No, I'm not all right. I can't... Are you mad?"

She coughed, trying to hold back the hysterical laughter building inside of her, but she couldn't. Loud, painful giggles bubbled out of her mouth. He was her last chance, and if he didn't agree, she'd have to think of another plan.

"This isn't funny," he said. His brown eyes were dark and piercing as they raked over her.

Trying without success to hold back more giggles, she said, "I know it isn't."

But she couldn't quit laughing, and it wasn't a joyous laugh. It was painful, degrading, and utterly horrifying that she had to ask. She wasn't even sure this would solve her problem, but it was the only solution she'd thought of in the past few days. The only idea that didn't make her want to hurl her last meal all over the ground.

"Then why are you laughing?" he said.

"I'm laughing because if I don't... I might cry." *Oh, why did I just say that?*

His gaze bored into hers, searching, probing. He knew her well, but he likely would've never expected this from her. She would have never expected this from herself, but her options were gone. Suddenly, his expression softened.

Her skin tingled with a fierce longing she thought she had suppressed years ago. This was supposed to be a business arrangement. Nothing more, nothing less. She had loved Cole for years, but he'd never seen her as anything more than his best friend and employer.

"Why would you ask me to do this? I don't understand," he said.

"What is there to understand?" She straightened her spine with resolve. "I want a child. This seems the obvious solution. You're discreet and won't hurt me. I thought you would help."

Cole stood and paced in front of the fire, clutching an embroidered pillow. He looked large and menacing compared to the daintiness of the pink pillow. He moved closer to her, but she stood her ground. She wasn't afraid of him, but from the look in his eyes, she wondered if she had gone too far.

"You aren't married. What would people think?"

"I don't care. It's none of their business." This was risky, but she'd considered all the possibilities. In the end, no one would know because she'd disappear as soon as she confirmed a baby was in her womb.

"It isn't right. You'll be ostracized. The child would be a... a..." He stopped his pacing, his gaze intense.

She stood her ground. "I think the word you're looking for is *bastard*."

His eyes narrowed. "Frannie――"

"Don't say it." If he refused her, she'd be even more embarrassed than she already was.

"You don't know what you're asking," he said, his tone low.

"Of course I do. I'm not a young girl anymore. I'm twenty-eight. There isn't a man in this town who wants me for anything but my money." Her toes curled. This was humiliating, but she had to make him understand. "I want someone who cares for me, and I won't settle for less. But I'm getting older, and before long, I won't be able to have any children. I want――No. I *need* a child. Father made sure I'd be taken care of, and no one in this town would dare besmirch any child of mine, for fear of what I could do, and you know it." She spoke with bravado and knew she'd be considered a pariah, but it wouldn't serve her to admit that.

"That isn't the point. You aren't thinking rationally." He threw the pillow across the room, where it hit the wall with a soft thud before fluttering to the ground.

"Don't tell me what I'm thinking. I want a child." Her voice grew belligerent. She had asked a simple question. He only needed to say yes or no. He didn't need to drag out her mortification.

"I understand you do," he said, his eyes sad.

"Do you? Because if you did, you'd agree." Her fingernails dug into her palms. She'd likely have marks when this was all said and done.

"What you're asking is... is ridiculous. We're friends. I work for you. I can't..."

"You can. You have all the working parts, right? I've been told you visit the brothel regularly, and the women say you're virile and not lacking in that department." She glanced at the juncture of his thighs and blushed at the memory of Laurie and her girls explaining his prowess. "In fact, Laurie told me you perform to such a satisfying degree that she has to stop the girls from fighting over you. I'm surprised there aren't twenty little Coles running around town right now."

He stared at her incredulously. "Why in the world are you having conversations with harlots?" He stalked to the far wall and picked up the pillow he'd thrown moments before.

She might be single in a male-dominated world, but women talked, and she listened. She'd been determined to know all she needed before she approached him with something that should have happened between her and her future husband. But the man she wanted didn't want her, at least not that way.

"I own almost every piece of property in town. Of course, I'm going to talk to the harlots."

He froze, his knuckles turning white as he squeezed the pink pillow. She was surprised the seams hadn't burst from the pressure.

"Are you planning on ripping my pillow to shreds?" she asked, trying to lighten the mood. The tension between them crackled like a wildfire, he with anger and disbelief and she with desire.

"What?" He looked at his hands. "Sorry, I didn't mean..."

"I know you didn't." She stepped close, the heat from his body warming her. If she weren't careful, she would burst into flames and explode at his feet. There was more than just her wanting a child. Perhaps if he saw her as the mother of his child, he'd see her as someone he could love too, but considering his horrified expression, that would never happen. She would have to settle for his baby if he agreed to her plan. She took the pillow from him and dropped it on the loveseat before placing her hand on his arm. "Please, Cole, I need this. I need *you*."

He yanked his arm away and stepped aside, putting distance between them. His face burned bright red. Her heart fell. It was still the same. Nothing would ever change. He would never look at her as more than his childhood friend, the one he'd played with, tormented, and encouraged once she became old enough to understand that she lived in a world that would never let her rule her own life, not without a man's help. When her father died, Cole had been the one to step in and protect her, even when she didn't want it, but now she wanted more.

"You can't ask me to do this. It isn't fair. You're not what I..."

"I'm not what? Sexy, beautiful, charming enough?" Her voice was tight with anger and frustration. It had come to this.

He slammed his fist against the wall. An oil painting trembled from the force of his blow. "I didn't say that. I work for you. You pay me. You tell me what to do every single day."

"That's irrelevant. I'm not telling you to do this. I'm asking you," she said. "I mean, isn't this what men do? Couple with women, get their pleasure and satisfaction, and then leave them to deal with the consequences? I know what those are, and I'm prepared to handle it."

"How would you know... Shit. What has Laurie told you?" He rubbed at his eyes, avoiding her gaze.

"Enough to know you would be perfect for what I need."

"You don't know that. You never have, and you never will. Your father gave you too much freedom and not enough proper direction," he snapped.

"How dare you? He has nothing to do with this." Her father had loved Cole as though he were his son and had always treated him well. He would've been disappointed to know Cole wouldn't help her when she needed it the most. Although he'd be appalled at what she was asking of him. No other options were left to her, and she was making the best decision she could.

"He has everything to do with this. If he were here..." Cole shook his head.

"He isn't here and hasn't been for quite some time." She stomped her foot in frustration. "I know what I want. If you aren't man enough to be there for me, then you can just leave." Her chest burned, her eyes brimming with tears she refused to let fall. "There are plenty of men who would love to have me in their bed if they thought they had any chance at my money. In fact, Henry Davenport has wanted me for years. I should've gone to him instead."

"Have you lost your mind?" he roared, his voice filled with a rage she had never seen or heard before.

She took a few steps back, covering her mouth with her palm.

"Henry's not the man for you."

"I'm not going to marry the man," she said. "I'm going to sleep with him until I'm with child."

"No, you aren't." His nostrils flared as he stalked toward her.

"You can't stop me," she said, her voice quivering. She wouldn't let him intimidate her. She had to have this baby. Her father's will demanded it. If she didn't have a child before her thirty-first birthday, everything he had worked so hard for would no longer be hers.

Somehow, Henry had discovered the details of her father's will. He knew if she didn't have a child, everything would go to Henry's father, George. What her father hadn't realized was that George would die mere months after her father did, leaving everything to Henry unless she had a baby.

Henry had threatened her the day before. He'd told her it would make more sense if she married him and had his child; otherwise, she would be left alone on the street, destitute, with nothing to show for herself other than the clothes on her back.

Cole straightened his shoulders and glared at her. "Yes, I can

stop you from sleeping with that despicable man. I have no choice.
I'll do it. Your father would be appalled if I let you anywhere near
Henry, but it'll be on my terms. Not yours."

"What do you mean by that?" This might have been a bad
idea. She didn't like the look in his eyes.

"You'll marry me," he said, glowering at her.

Her mouth fell open in shock. It took her a moment but she
gathered her composure. "No, I won't. We don't need to do that.
Laurie told me it doesn't take marriage to get a child in my belly."

He shook his head, sighing heavily after every word she
uttered.

"Laurie said you'll only need to sleep with me a time or two."
Her face was blazing hot.

He clenched the back of the loveseat and his fingers grew red
from the force. It was a wonder it didn't break from the force of
his grip.

Laurie had told her that sometimes it could take months,
depending on the woman and the virility of the man. She was sure
Cole would've stopped the negotiations right then if she told him
he might have to sleep with her over the course of a few months.
Laurie had even cackled with glee when Frannie revealed it was
Cole she wanted as the father of her child. "That man will get you
with child right quick, Miss Frannie, but if you're lucky, it won't."
Laurie winked. "And you'll get to enjoy him on more than one
occasion."

Frannie wasn't about to tell Cole what Laurie had said, she'd
keep that information to herself.

"I'm not going to sleep with you unless we are married," Cole
said.

"But, Cole—"

"Don't, Frannie." He clenched his teeth. "It isn't up for nego-
tiation. You'll marry me first."

Two

Cole strode down the dirt road to his home, a mere five houses from Frannie. He still couldn't believe he had agreed to bed her. Of all the women in town, why did it have to be her? She was his best friend, his employer, the person he confided in. He was sick to his stomach for agreeing to her cockamamy plan. *What the hell am I thinking?*

If she hadn't mentioned Henry, he might've been able to walk away unscathed, but as soon as she said the man's name, he'd known he had to do as she asked. Henry wanted Frannie, panted after her, talked about her behind closed doors with derision and disgust. He only wanted one thing, and that was the mine and all the money that came with it.

Frannie's father had left her well off, too well off, and with too much control over his estate. It wasn't common for a woman to have that much power, but Frank hadn't wanted her to suffer if he were to die before she married.

But something had changed. Henry had been strutting around for weeks, acting as though the coal mine would be his. Cole had tried talking to Frannie on numerous occasions, but she refused to discuss it with him. He feared there was something more behind her request but had no idea what it might be.

What Frannie didn't know was that Cole had noticed when she started looking at him as more than her best friend, her eyes trailing his whenever she didn't think he was looking. He even remembered the night before Frank had passed. Cole had come knocking on their door late at night, long after he was sure Frannie had gone to bed. He hadn't wanted to see her, but he'd needed to speak with Frank.

Frank had let him inside the house, his eyes solemn. "Cole, it's good to see you. Come in, come in." He'd stepped away, pushing the screen door back to usher Cole inside. "Would you care for a bite to eat?"

A pot of stew sat on the table, a thick loaf of bread and a crock of dark yellow butter next to it.

"No, thank you. I'm not hungry." His belly churned at the thought of eating. He didn't want to tell Frank what had happened, but he couldn't go another minute without telling him he'd kissed his precious daughter.

"How'd you like a cup of coffee, then?" Frank didn't look at him but poured a cup before he could agree and placed it on the table. "Sit, son."

Cole ripped off his woolen stocking hat, holding it tight between his fingers. He was uneasy that he'd disappoint Frank, and sweat built under his arms and down his back. This was a conversation he'd never wanted to have with the man who was a second father.

Slipping into the chair, he picked up the cup and held it between his fingers, took a sip, and then raised his eyes.

Frank sat across from him, leaning back in his chair. "Do you have something on your mind?"

He dropped the cup, and the hot liquid sloshed over his fingers. Cursing under his breath, he wiped his hands on his trousers. "Sorry, Frank. Didn't mean to be insulting."

Frank just smiled.

Cole pushed at his thighs. "I've got something to tell you.

"I'm sure you do," Frank said. "You look like you've swallowed a canary."

His mouth had grown dry like he'd just chewed a handful of leavened crackers. "Um... well, I should've come to you sooner, but I... well, I..." He couldn't do this. He was going to be sick.

Shoving his hands against the table, he pushed away and stumbled to stand.

Frank's chair scooted back. "Sit, Cole. I know what happened."

Cole hadn't wanted Frank to find out before he'd had a chance to tell him.

Doing as Frank demanded, Cole sat but averted his gaze.

"Frannie came home this afternoon, her face red, streaks of dried tears on her cheeks. It was as though she'd lost her favorite puppy."

Cole hadn't wanted to hurt her, but he had. "I know. It's my fault." Cole was sure Frank would fire him if he didn't wring his scrawny neck first.

Frank chuckled, the sound bouncing across the room. "It ain't your fault, son."

Cole raised his head. "I'm the cause of her tears."

"No, you ain't." Frank rubbed his chin. "Frannie's held a torch for you for years. When she told me she'd kissed you and that you didn't return her affections, she was mortified she'd placed you in that position."

"She told you that?"

"Yes, she did. She didn't want you to feel guilty for what she believed she had done."

Cole stared at Frank and saw the compassion in his eyes. Frank knew how Cole felt and how he'd decided years ago that he would never marry, never have children after he'd watched his parents' marriage fall apart. His ma had treated his pa abominably, sleeping with every man who'd shown her the slightest interest, while his pa had worked hard in the coal mine, trying his utmost to get them out of the poverty they found themselves in. Eventually, his ma had run off with a smarmy salesman when Cole was ten years old, not giving Cole and his sister a second glance as she packed up her belongings and fled. She hadn't been concerned with her children. Thankfully, when he discovered his wife had passed away years later, Cole's pa had picked up the pieces and married a widow who had a son. She'd tried to care for Cole and his sister, but Cole had never trusted his new ma would stay.

That next morning, Cole was to meet Frank at the mine. When Frank didn't arrive, Cole had gone looking for him.

"Frank," he'd said, knocking on the door.

"No!" Frannie screamed and it'd sent chills down his spine.

Cole rushed inside and down the hall. He scrambled to a stop when he found Frannie rocking back and forth on the floor, her father's body in her arms.

"Frannie," he'd said, his throat closing.

She raised her head and the look of despair on her face had near broken him in half. Her father was gone.

The memories of that night and the subsequent morning were ones he couldn't forget, and he had to remember what he had promised Frank. He was bound to protect her, although he'd never expected the protection would involve him marrying Frannie. With one request from her, he'd agreed to go against everything he held dear just to keep her safe from Henry Davenport.

What stuck in his craw was that she'd used Henry as a bargaining chip. Now that he had calmed his nerves, he was sure Frannie had used that intentional argument to get what she wanted, but did she even know what she wanted or what she was getting?

He was caught between a rock and a stonemason's chisel. He didn't want to bed her or marry her, but if he didn't, then she would turn to Henry, and that was something he could not fathom or agree to, not while he had breath left in his body.

Their negotiations had been strange. She'd refused to marry him until she was sure she was with child. He wasn't sure he should've agreed, but it gave him an out, and she knew that. At least they were friends, and he could stomach being around her. No child of his would be fatherless or called a bastard. He just wished she had agreed to the marriage before they slept together, but she'd been insistent she wouldn't marry until she was with child. He still wasn't sure it was a good idea, but he'd agreed. Now the only thing left was to actually perform the act.

She had wanted to get it over with, but he needed time to convince himself he could do it. It wasn't that Frannie was unattractive. She was the most beautiful woman he knew, both inside and out, with her kind nature and her generosity to those less fortunate than herself. There were plenty of times when she left baskets of food on the porches of the poorest families in town, and most didn't know it came from her. But he had never looked at her in that way, never allowed himself to do so because she was his friend and could never be more than that. The potential heartbreak was too great. There was no guarantee things would work out for the best, and it suited him to be on his own.

"Cole."

He turned. A friend and one of the foremen from the mine ran up to him. Cole's memories of the past needed to stay where they were. He had responsibilities and couldn't be distracted.

"Hello there, Jacob."

"You got a minute, boss?" Jacob braced his hands against his knees to catch his breath. He was a big man, and his large body had lumbered pretty quick, but he was now winded. He must've run a fair distance to be this out of sorts.

"For you, anytime."

"We got a problem at the mine." Jacob had been working at the mine since he returned from the war. He'd rather be out West, though, and been saving every penny he had in order to leave Pennsylvania and head toward the open and vast areas that were begging to be explored. Jacob had told him when he signed on that he was close to having the money he needed, and with any luck, he'd be leaving Pennsylvania soon. Cole didn't want his friend to leave, but he understood why.

"What now?" There'd been nonstop problems in the coal mine as of late, and he didn't need more bad news, least of all today.

Taking a breath, Jacob stood tall. "We lost the roof in the east mine."

"Shit!" Cole ran a hand through his hair, scratching at the back of his scalp. "Was anyone killed?" He didn't need this and prayed no one had died.

"No, thank the heavens above."

Jacob fell in step beside Cole as they turned back toward another unfortunate incident in the wake of too many. Cole was worried the mishaps weren't accidental––that someone was trying to cause harm.

"No one was in the shaft when it happened, but we've got a bigger problem. Huggar and his crew are starting their rumblings again and are insisting the mine conditions are unsafe."

"What does that man expect now?" Huggar was a pain in his backside and had been for months. If Cole didn't know better, he'd think Huggar was causing the accidents. Frannie had men coming at her from all sides, and there was only so much he could do.

"Not sure, but with this latest collapse, you know he's gonna get more support. Huggar's insisting Miss Collins is irresponsible and shouldn't own the mine. He thinks she should sell it to him and his band of warriors. He believes he could make it safer for everyone and that no woman is gonna tell him what to do."

"You know she'll never do that, and she shouldn't have to." His strides were long and sure, and before long, they'd reached the mine's main office building. Men milled in groups, looking fit to be tied. He was going to have a riot on his hands if these unexplained accidents didn't stop.

"I know you believe she shouldn't be in charge," Jacob said, his voice low. "Maybe you could talk to her, tell her how dangerous things are gettin'."

Cole had told Jacob that in confidence one night when they had too much to drink, but he wasn't wrong. Frank had made the wrong decision leaving the mine to his daughter. She wasn't strong enough to handle the discord among the men. She tried, but they didn't respect her and thought she should be at home raising babes. Cole thought she should do the same, but she knew more about the mine than any man there, including him.

Frannie had followed her pa around from the time she could walk, reading everything she could get her hands on, always listening and learning. The problem was her pa wasn't there to protect her any longer, and the men had grown discontent and angry in the four years since he'd passed. The latest string of accidents had caused even more resentment and envy among the men. Cole wasn't sure how much longer she'd be able to hold on to it without someone causing her harm.

"Jacob, you know I don't want anyone knowing that."

Jacob put his hand on Cole's arm, bringing them both to a stop. "I know you're her friend, and you promised her father you would look out for her, but this has gotten volatile. The men are angry. There have been too many accidents of late, and it doesn't appear she's doing anything."

"You know much of this is out of her control. It's the nature of mining."

"You know that, and I know that, but it doesn't matter anymore." Jacob held up his hand. "You might be on her side, but she's gonna get hurt if you don't do something."

"I can't force her to give up the mine. Let me talk to the men——"

"The men aren't gonna listen. If she doesn't sell and sell soon, we're gonna have a mutiny on our hands. This town can't sustain that kind of disruption. The last time it happened, it almost ruined this town and the people in it."

"It was her father who saved it, don't you forget." Frank had almost lost everything when Frannie was just a child, but he'd been determined to make things right for the families in town and had done so. He'd been a beloved member of the community when he swooped in and rescued many families from the poorhouse, but once he passed away and the men learned Frannie owned everything, things had deteriorated.

"I know, but memories are short. They don't want a woman to tell 'em what to do. You've got to convince her to sell."

"I don't know," Cole said.

"If she had a husband, that'd stop the anger in its tracks." Jacob grinned, and it lifted his cheeks. He'd always believed Cole would make Frannie a fine husband and had told Cole that on many occasions.

"Maybe, but she doesn't want to get married. The men who've tried to court her have only been after her money, and she knows that."

Jacob's smile had disappeared. "That may be true, but she may just have to accept that. Otherwise, things are gonna get dangerous soon."

They reached the mine and found men covered in coal soot, standing in circles, anger, desperation, and fear on their faces.

"Hey, Seymour. Whatcha gonna do about this latest accident?" a man yelled. It was Huggar. He was short and stocky, with thick arms from swinging a pickax day in and day out. Huggar and his cronies were sullen, and it wouldn't take much to set them off.

Cole shook his head. Things were boiling over. "You let me worry about that."

Huggar threw him a dirty look before turning back to his friends, their hisses of anger and discontent clear even if Cole couldn't hear everything they said.

"That proves my point," Jacob whispered. "They're angry and won't be satisfied unless a man is running things."

"I am running things," Cole snapped.

"You may tell the men what to do, but she calls the shots, and everyone knows it."

Jacob was right, no matter how much Cole wanted to deny it. "There's no point in debating this any further. I'll talk to her. In the meantime, we need to get the shaft closed off and check the ones close by to make sure the rest are stable."

"I already took care of it. I sent men to check the supports to make sure we don't have a bigger problem. They'll clean out the shaft once we know it's secure."

"Thanks, Jacob. You're a godsend. Frannie's lucky to have you." Cole gripped his friend's shoulder for a long moment. "I'll be back in an hour. I'll tell Frannie what happened and see if I can't get her to consider selling."

Jacob nodded, then left Cole staring off into the distance at the mine that was causing all the ruckus. Cole slapped his hat back on his head and rested his hands on his hips. The last thing he wanted to do was go back to Frannie's after their conversation this morning, but it looked like he didn't have a choice. She needed to sell the mine or get married.

Marriage seemed the practical choice, but he wasn't sure either of them would be happy with it. Her insistence that they wouldn't marry unless she became pregnant told him she wasn't all that keen on the idea to begin with. But maybe with the threat of losing control of the men, she'd reconsider. He just wished it wasn't him being the proverbial lamb being offered to the lion as dinner.

~

Hours after Cole had left, Frannie lay chest-deep in her tub. The hot water, bath salts, and thick white bubbles calmed her frayed nerves. Her hair was piled high on her head, wet strands lining her cheeks. She reclined lazily with her left knee bent and her left arm resting on the edge, while her right hand stroked and molded the foam in front of her. As her mind drifted, she leaned her head back, closed her eyes, and placed a warm cloth over them. She should get out before her skin wrinkled, but she enjoyed her baths and would stay until the water grew tepid. Talking with Cole about what she wanted had been an emotional challenge but one she didn't regret. Better for her to ask and face rejection than to stew about it for the rest of her life.

A knock sounded on the bathroom door.

"Come in." The tingle of the teakettle echoed behind her. "You can put the tray on the table, Carrie."

A faint thud sounded when the tray was dropped. Carrie always knew what to bring her.

"Thank you," she murmured.

"My pleasure." It was a deep masculine voice.

She wrenched the cloth from her eyes and sat. The water sloshed over the sides of the tub as she snapped her neck sideways to see who had entered her sanctuary. She sighed. "What the hell are you doing in here?"

"Bringing you your tea." Cole leaned against the brown window frame, his face devoid of expression. The white lace curtains fluttered from the breeze.

She didn't know what he was thinking, but he didn't need to see her like this. "Get out." She pointed toward the door.

"Now, why are you being so unfriendly?" He grinned, lifting a finger to push back a lock of brown hair that had fallen across his eye. "I'm going to see every inch of your body if we're to get you with child." His voice was low and sensuous, sending shivers up her spine. His eyes twinkled, and he slowly folded his arms across his chest, his gaze sending a rush of heat to every inch of her skin.

Something had changed, but she wasn't sure what. "I said, get out." She rose partly out of the water, and the water sloshed across her skin.

He uncrossed his arms and strode toward her. She sank into the water, prayed the bubbles would shield the deep red blush that covered her from head to toe, and tried without success to hide her breasts from his unflinching gaze.

He stood over her, tall, strong, and oozing masculinity, before he placed his hands on the edge of the tub and bent until his face was near hers. "I think we need to talk."

She didn't blink. "We spoke earlier. There's nothing more to say."

"Oh, there's plenty to say, and things have changed. Marriage is your only choice unless you want to lose the mine and have a mutiny on your hands."

"What do you mean?" She sat up, forgetting she was naked as the day she was born. "The mine has nothing to do with our agreement."

"Maybe not before, but it certainly does now."

Three

Cole's heart thundered in his chest. He didn't know what the hell he'd been thinking. Walking into her bathing room, catching her wearing nothing but a thick cover of bubbles that disappeared when the water splashed over the edges. He'd been so focused on letting her know what had happened at the mine that it didn't even occur to him that she could be naked.

There had been no doubt about her beauty, but seeing her with her thick blonde hair in a messy knot and wet curls nestled against her long neck, he lost all sense of himself.

Carrie had waved him upstairs when he caught her carrying the tray of tea. She looked tired and harried and hadn't given it a second thought when he took it from her hands and told her he would deliver it to Frannie. She either hadn't known Frannie was taking a bath or hadn't cared. Either way, he'd found Frannie in a compromising position. He justified it to himself since they were to be married, but it gave him a moment of pause.

He had never seen her as more than a friend, but things were different, and he didn't know why. It had been happening slowly over the past few months, creeping up on him like a caterpillar stretching in the afternoon sun. It didn't matter how his body and mind reacted. Determined to keep her at arm's length, he'd succeeded until she approached him that very morning with her rash plan.

Getting a rise out of her wasn't helping, but he couldn't help himself. Her cheeks were pink, her breasts full and heavy as she sat straight up in the tub. Indignant at his comment, she either hadn't realized she'd done it or no longer cared. Either way, he was going to enjoy every moment, even if she was spitting mad.

Common sense prevailed, and he reached for a towel to remove the temptation of taking her right then and there. She snatched it from his fingertips, wrapped it around her naked body, and climbed out of the tub, sputtering while he told her about the mine and Huggar's latest threat.

She ignored the water dripping from her skin as she stood on the tiled floor, her toes curling from the chill in the air, and secured the towel around her breasts. She pushed strands of hair from her cheeks. "Huggar won't get the mine. I'll never sell to him."

"Things are getting volatile, out of control." He followed her into her bedroom, one he had spent plenty of time in as a young boy. He hadn't crossed the threshold once she had changed from a plump little girl to a cute young woman to the striking and gorgeous woman she was now. "You won't have a choice."

She stomped over to her dressing screen, the scent of roses lingering in the air. Whatever she used had always intrigued him. If he was going to marry her, he was going to find out what it was, where she put it, and how he could buy more so she'd always smell that delicious.

"Of course, I have a choice."

She said more, but he couldn't tell what it was. The screen muffled her voice.

"I can't hear you, Frannie." He watched her silhouette halt.

She slapped the towel over the top of the screen and peeked her head around the side, her fingers gripping it. "I said"––her voice was huffy, as though he should have had his ears against the screen to hear every word she uttered--"it's my mine. I won't give in to those radicals. Huggar has been a thorn in my side for years. You told me to let it go when Father died and that he would stop harassing me." Her voice had risen with irritation and angst. She turned, giving him a glimpse of her slim waist and round backside.

The heat inside his belly expanded, and the seam of his trousers brushed against the intensifying bulge between his legs. He knew how to rein in his ardor, but something about her pushed away the slim control he held on to.

Praying his voice wouldn't squeak like an adolescent boy, he swallowed a few times. "Frannie, I know, but—"

"No buts. I'm not selling to that piece of shit."

He chuckled. "Your language is getting quite fierce."

"Oh, shut up." Her voice cracked with tears.

Cole walked toward the screen, but she had moved farther behind it, pulling on her clothes, when she slapped the wall and muffled a cry of distress.

"Don't cry..."

"I'm not crying," she snapped, coming from around the screen wearing a white cotton petticoat and corset. She had been yanking on the strings but stopped in front of him and slapped the ties into his hands. Placing her hands on her hips, she turned. "Pull those, will you?" As though him helping her get dressed was a normal occurrence.

He fumbled with the ties but did as she asked. His gaze roamed across her slim shoulders and over to the swells of her breasts that rose and fell with each breath she took. This was dangerous, and he should leave, but his feet were frozen in place.

"I'm not going to sell."

"Then we need to come up with another plan."

She huffed when he pulled the strings too tight.

"Sorry," he muttered.

"Don't apologize. Pull tighter." She turned her head and

looked at him over her shoulder. "The plan is to fire that worthless piece of cow dung. Get him off my property and out of my mines."

"That's risky." After tugging one more time, he tied the strings and rested his hands on her tiny waist. While he appreciated a woman's curves, the corsets they wore made their waists too small. What he'd seen of her figure didn't need improvement. He'd seen the lines corsets would leave on the harlots he visited. He couldn't imagine what this one was doing to Frannie's already perfect body.

"No, it isn't." She glared at him, then stalked to her wardrobe and yanked it open before slamming it closed. "I want him gone. If you don't fire him today, I'll do it myself." Stomping to her vanity, she reached for a comb, pulled out the hairpins, and ran the metal comb through the long strands.

Cole had a battle on his hands. She wouldn't listen to reason. "Firing him won't solve the discontent. If you do that, you're just going to anger those who support him."

She slapped the comb onto the table. "Then fire them. There are plenty of men who need jobs, who would be happy to work for me. I'm tired of kowtowing to those ungrateful ingrates. Without my father's selfless deeds, Huggar wouldn't have a job. He'd have nothing."

"That isn't true, and you know it." She was letting her anger override her good sense. He walked to her side and took her hands. She tried to wrench them away, but he held fast. "We've had a hard time keeping men because you own it."

"That's ridiculous." Her brilliant green eyes shined with unshed tears. She sniffled, then straightened her back as though she had a steel rod jammed up her backside. "I'll... I'll just increase the pay, offer them more. Times are hard. If we make it worthwhile, they'll be happy for the work."

He shook his head and lowered his voice. "No, they won't. I did that. It hasn't worked."

"What are you talking about?" She wrenched her hands away,

looked in the vanity's mirror, and twisted her hair into a tight knot at the base of her neck, shoving hairpins to hold it in place.

He didn't want to tell her everything, but maybe he had kept her in the dark for too long. "I've been increasing the men's pay for months, trying to keep them on, trying to hire more, but it isn't working. The war took many good men, as you well know, and what's left ain't much to cheer about." He rubbed the back of his neck. "The only reason Huggar hasn't left is because he has an ulterior motive. I'm afraid he's in cahoots with Henry Davenport and that they've been the ones causing the accidents. They both want the mine, especially now. Solid businesses that weren't torn apart by the war are rare, and they want it. I'd bet on my last dollar that Henry has promised Huggar something. If Huggar leaves, he loses that leverage, and neither man will do that."

"Why haven't you said anything?" Her eyes flashed dangerously.

He winced at her censure. He'd kept the growing incidents from her and was ashamed to admit he hadn't been able to find the source. "I was trying to keep things from falling apart."

She poked a finger into his chest. "You should have said something, told me."

He brushed her hand away. "It wouldn't have done any good. You couldn't have changed it."

"I could have..." She dropped into the chair in front of her vanity. "What am I going to do? I can't lose everything Father worked so hard for."

She started shaking. He knelt in front of her, but she swatted at his hands.

"Don't touch me." Her voice quivered. He ignored her and scooped her up in his arms. "What are you doing?" she screeched.

She tried to fight him, but he didn't let go, and after a moment, she stopped. Frannie clung to him and buried her face in his shoulder, tears soaking his shirt. He sat on the edge of her bed, holding her close as she silently cried.

After a few minutes, she stopped. He handed her a handkerchief. She wiped her face with the soft, white cotton and then blew her nose, the sound loud and unladylike. It made him want to chuckle. She wasn't afraid to be herself in front of him, and that was one of many qualities that made his gut twinge at the thought of her being with anyone else. That was why he would be the one to marry and bed her. There was no way in hell he would ever let Henry near her, not if she was insisting on carrying through with her plan.

"What should I do?" Her heart was on her sleeve, her eyes begging for a solution.

Cole shouldn't have kept things from her for as long as he had. He'd believed he was doing the right thing, but he had miscalculated.

He sighed and adjusted her in his lap. His fingers grazed across her soft skin. "Your only choice is to marry. If you have a husband, they'll have nothing to complain about."

"And who is going to marry me?" She pushed his hand away and tried to move, but he kept her in place. "Every man who has shown any interest has only been after my pa's money, and you know it. I can't marry someone who'll ruin my father's legacy."

"Marry me." As much as the thought of being shackled in marriage frightened him, he couldn't let her make a colossal mistake. "I know we discussed this, but if you marry me now instead of waiting to see if you're with child, you and the mine'll be safe from Henry and Huggar."

Her soft body nestled perfectly in his lap, and he wanted to keep her there. His feelings were scattered. One minute, he wanted to marry her and give her the baby she wanted. The next, he was fearful he would lose himself like his pa had, that she would find she couldn't be married to him and leave him as his ma had.

"You don't want to marry me," she said. "I saw your face when I asked you to give me a baby. You didn't want to do that, so I'm positive you don't want to tie yourself to me. Besides, you've steered away from courting any woman in town. I know you aren't interested in the bonds of marriage."

She wasn't wrong, but it was the only way to save what was hers. He had made promises to her father, and if this was the only way to keep her safe, then he would swallow his misgivings and marry her. But he only had one chance to convince her, and this was it. "You agreed to marry me earlier if you became pregnant. We'll just move up the timeline. We'll marry and then try for a child."

"No," she said, scrambling off his lap. Her breathing had intensified. "I can't marry you, ever."

It was as though a dagger had just been shoved into his heart. *What is wrong with me?* "That isn't what you agreed to earlier."

"Well, I lied." She avoided his gaze.

"No child of mine will be without a father or be labeled as a bastard."

"It doesn't matter now. Nothing matters." Her voice was filled with anguish.

He didn't like where this conversation was going. "Come here, Frannie."

"No. You need to leave and tell Huggar he's fired. I don't want him on my property any longer. I don't care what he's threatened. Until I'm dead, Father's mine belongs to me."

He grabbed her by the elbow.

"Let me go."

"No." Without another conscious thought, he pulled her into his arms and kissed her. Clearly stunned, she didn't move for a few seconds before she whimpered, curling her arms around his neck, and sighing with pleasure.

He deepened the kiss, molding her lips to his while his hands rose up her corseted back, skimming the sides, inching toward her smooth skin. She shivered and pulled him closer before moaning deep in her throat, caressing the back of his neck. His hair stood on end, and goose bumps prickled his exposed forearms.

Before he could stop himself, he twisted and dropped her onto the thick quilts of her bed. Her petticoats fluttered near her waist, exposing her long, bare legs. She hadn't put on any stockings and only wore a petticoat. Not even drawers adorned her backside. His heart thudded in his chest, his hands grew sweaty, and his groin tightened. He wanted her with a fierceness that surprised him.

He shouldn't do this. He was taking advantage of her vulnerable state, but she didn't stop him or warn him off. He needed to be one hundred percent certain this was what she wanted as his cock throbbed, aching for release with a mind all of its own. He couldn't let it take control of his mind, for if he did, he might never stop.

He touched her bare foot, running his finger against the arch. She squealed but didn't pull away from his touch.

"Are you sure?" he asked.

No words came from her lips, but her head nodded just enough that, if he hadn't been eyeing her closely, he would've missed the slight movement. She didn't cover herself and held as still as a church mouse, clutching the quilt beneath her. Frannie waited for him, and he couldn't resist.

Cole bent and pulled off his boots, one by one. Her eyes watched his every move. He flicked open his shirt, one button at a time, giving her the option to change her mind. Cole shrugged out of it, letting it fall behind him. He reached for his belt buckle when she scooted back on the bed, pulling a pillow to her chest. He paused. While he craved her touch, he wouldn't do more than she wanted.

She swallowed, her chest rising and falling as if she had run from the mine.

"I can stop," he said.

She shook her head and licked her plump lips, moisture glistening across them. Heat soared through him. His trousers constricted what he wanted to release, and he couldn't keep it contained much longer. He unbuckled his belt and shoved his trousers over his hips. Stepping out of them, he stood in front of her, his cock jutting out, just begging for her touch.

"Frannie, are you sure you want this?"

"Yes," she murmured and moved the pillow to the side before she ran her fingers across the swell of her breasts. Her breath hitched as she eyed him like a piece of cherry pie.

He climbed onto the bed next to her, and she rolled toward him. She was a sensuous vixen in just her corset, petticoat, and chemise. Nothing fancy, just plain white cotton, but she looked enticing in the ensemble. She could wear a potato sack, and she'd still be beautiful.

Cole placed one hand on her corset and supported his head with his other. She shivered as he traced the curves of her body, his fingers having a mind of their own as he moved along her soft skin.

"You truly are lovely," he whispered.

She turned her head, her cheeks bright red. "Do all men talk while they're doing this?" She waved a hand in the air.

He chuckled, and her face scrunched.

"Don't laugh at me," she mumbled.

"I'm not laughing at you, I promise."

She raised her hand and cupped his cheek, her palm warm against his skin. Lust surged through him, bubbling and boiling to the surface. He wanted to rip off her clothing and taste her sweet essence. While he knew what to do and generally coupled with women who did as well, Frannie had never been with a man, and he'd do well to remember that. She was innocent in the ways of the marriage bed.

The marriage bed!

He should stop. He needed to marry her before he bed her. It was the right thing to do.

Cole removed his hand from her skin and scooted back, but before he could climb out of the bed, she grabbed him by the shoulders and pulled him close. Her plump lips took his in another soul-searing kiss that sent a blaze of sensation to every inch of his skin. He nipped at her lower lip, sucking, tasting, groaning in her mouth. Their hot breath mingled when he finally pulled away and rested his forehead against hers.

"We shouldn't do this..." He inhaled sharply as she ran her hands across his chest, her fingers gentle as they brushed against his nipples. They tightened, and his cock pulsated in anticipation. His heart pounded in his chest, and desire surged through his body. He lifted his free hand and lightly touched her breasts.

She muttered his name, her legs and body sliding across the bedcovers as though searching for something not yet attained. He knew what she needed, and his excitement grew at giving her that and more.

He yanked at the corset he had tightened around her waist and exposed her nipples to his lips. His tongue lapped at one and then the other. She jumped under him before he pulled one tight, swirling his tongue until the bud hardened.

Cole couldn't wait to find out how she would respond to everything else he'd do to her. He would make her sing with pleasure if it was the last thing he ever did and would die happy knowing he had brought her satisfaction. Dragging his hand down her side, he nudged her thighs apart, searching for her soft center. The dark blonde curls beckoned his touch. Opening the folds with his fingers, wetness moistened his fingertips. He had done little, and she was already damp. Suddenly, she pushed at his hands.

He hesitated, lifted his head from her breast, and looked into her deep green eyes. "Do you want me to stop?"

"What are you doing?"

His head swam with needy anticipation, but he had to proceed with caution. She didn't know what was going to happen, and he had to prepare her both physically and emotionally.

"Do you know how a woman comes to be with a child?" He ran his fingers across her cheek, pushing strands of hair behind her ear.

A dark red blush rushed up her chest and into her cheeks. "Not exactly," she murmured.

"Laurie didn't tell you the specifics?" He thought for sure if she had spoken with the harlot, Frannie would know exactly what was to happen.

"She told me that you would show me what to do?" Her mouth pursed into a frown.

He wanted to chuckle but didn't think she'd appreciate that. Trying to come up with an example she might understand, he said, "Have you ever seen a horse mate or perhaps two dogs?"

"Ohhh," she said, understanding lighting her eyes. "But don't they... I mean, it's a different position... Oh heavens, how does this work?"

He picked up her hand, her fingers delicate between his, and guided them to between his legs. He twitched, so eager for her touch that it was painful. It was a wonder he didn't detonate like a stick of dynamite. Instead, a grunt slipped past his lips.

She yanked her hand away. "I'm sorry. I didn't mean to hurt you."

He bowed his head, closed his eyes, and took a few deep breaths. "You didn't hurt me."

"But you sounded as though you were in pain."

"That wasn't pain, my sweet. That... that was desire." His voice was hoarse.

"Oh." She giggled. "So, my touching you"––she lowered her eyes and looked straight at his cock, pushing against her skin–– "brings you pleasure?"

"Yes, it does."

A moment later, she wrapped her fingers around him, and he almost exploded. He pulled her hand away before he lost full control of his body.

"What are you doing? I wanted to touch you."

Intertwining his fingers with hers, he lifted his body and

climbed between her legs. "While I love that you've touched me there, I'm afraid if you do much more, you won't enjoy it."

"I don't understand." She scrunched her forehead as though trying to comprehend what he was trying to tell her.

"My seed will come on all of your fingers instead of in your womb." He let go of her hand and pointed to her belly. "You won't get pregnant if we do that. Do you want me to show you or tell you what's going to happen next?"

She looked at him for a long moment. "Show me. I want you to continue what you were doing. I want––No, I need you to continue. I want to have a child."

His heart seized with sadness and regret. While he had asked, he hadn't wanted the answer. She didn't want him. She wanted a baby. He was a means to an end.

When they spoke earlier in the day, he'd thought of their arrangement as a business one. It had been the only way he would have agreed, but now he wanted more. He wanted her to want him. He wanted to give her pleasure, make her scream with excitement, but not this way. "Are you wanting me only because this will get you with child?"

Her eyes wrinkled with confusion. She raised her hands to her face and covered her eyes. He sighed. She didn't know what she wanted, and he'd be damned if he took an innocent who wasn't prepared for what this meant.

He rose onto his knees and drew away. This would not be happening today. She wasn't ready for him, wasn't ready for this.

"Where are you going?" she cried, lifting onto her elbows, her lips puffy from his exploration, her breasts begging for him to continue.

"Damnit, Frannie. What are we doing? I can't do this to you."

She scrambled to her knees and grabbed him by the upper arms, keeping him from moving. "No, Cole. Don't leave me, not like this."

"We aren't being smart about this. You deserve to be married before I or any man takes your innocence. Besides, you said you would never marry me, so what is in this for me?"

"You've never wanted to be married. Why are you insisting on it now?"

"Because..." *Why am I doing this?* "Because your pa would've been disappointed."

She pushed her hair out of her face, reached behind her back, and before he could stop her, she ripped her corset off and lifted her chemise up and over her head, leaving her clad in only her petticoat.

"Frannie, stop!" She was making it very difficult to refuse her, and he didn't know how much control he really had.

She climbed onto his lap, straddled him, wrapped her arms around his neck, and placed her breasts against his chest. He should stop her, but he didn't want to. She was offering him something sweet and wonderful, and he was a fool to deny himself.

"Yes, we can do this, Cole Seymour. I want you. You want me. There's no reason we have to stop. None at all."

He capitulated and ravaged her with his lips, his pent-up need overriding his good sense. All reason disappeared with the thought of making her his. She trusted him, but it was difficult to remember she was untouched with her unbridled enthusiasm. She ran her hands across his body, discovering every inch of him as much, if not more so, than the discovery he did of her.

Before long, he slid inside her moist heat. It had been a long time since he had been with someone so perfect. Her eyes lit with pleasure, and moans of passion released from her lips. When they both reached a delightfully pleasurable peak, his heart sang with a joy he never thought possible. Moments later, his eyes closed, his arms wrapped tight around her supple body as he fell into a dreamless sleep.

Cole had never felt anything so wonderful, and he wanted to savor it for as long as possible.

Four

When Frannie woke, it was late, and she wasn't alone. Cole was curled next to her, his arm resting across her waist, his hand just under her breast. Her heart hurt, as she knew this was the first and last time she would ever be with him. He meant everything to her, but she didn't mean a thing to him. He might have insisted they were to marry, but she could never marry him. She wanted him to love her, but he never would, and she wasn't willing to accept anything less.

She thought she would've had a few weeks to implement her plans before sleeping with him. The last thing she'd expected was to spend the night with him, but now, with Henry and Huggar threatening her, all of her plans had been thrown out the window. Frannie had to sell as many properties as possible before anyone noticed she was with child, but she was assuming the one time would be all that was needed. She was putting all of her hopes in one moment with Cole. With any luck, she would be. If not, well, she'd have to live without having a child, for she could never sleep with another man. Cole had ruined her for anyone else. His touch had been hot and gentle, caressing her incessantly toward an inferno that built to an unexpected but fully satisfying crescendo.

She was completely and utterly in love with Cole and always had been.

Frannie brushed away the tears that sneaked from under her lids. No matter how much she tried to convince herself that there could be another man for her, it never worked. Cole was who she dreamed about, whose voice sent chills down her spine, whose every gaze made her swoon with desire, and whose touch had been everything and more. She wanted more time with him, but it wasn't possible, not any longer.

Frannie inched out from underneath his muscular arm and scooted off the bed. Tiptoeing to the chair next to the wall, she pulled on her wrapper. Brushing her hair off her face, she looked back at Cole. With his dark lashes framing his cheeks, he looked so peaceful in sleep, much different from how he had looked hours earlier.

His smoldering gaze was imprinted on her mind. He'd made her feel things she didn't think were possible. Her hands went to her belly. Perhaps she had finally gotten her wish. She shook her head. The unrealistic dreams needed to stop. Laurie said she might not conceive on the first try. It could happen, but because she was so much older, the chances were slim, but it wouldn't stop her from hoping.

Cole stirred and slid under the white sheets, patting the bed as though looking for something. A part of her hoped it was her, but she knew better. She was just a warm body that had given him a pleasurable release. Frannie was no worse and no better than the women who worked for Laurie, giving the man what he wanted while taking what she needed at the same time.

She stood silent, memorizing his features. This would be the last time she would ever see him this way. His eyes fluttered open, and the dark brown pupils deepened with desire. His stare was piercing, questioning, and something else she couldn't name and wasn't sure she wanted to, for she feared it was disgust.

He pushed up on his elbows. The sheets fell low across his

hips, and he seemed unconcerned with his undress. She blushed when he caught her eyeing him like he was a ripe peach that she wanted to suck until he quivered under her touch.

He raised an eyebrow, and a touch of a smile lifted on his lips. "Are you--"

"I'm fine." *What else am I supposed to say? That you were everything I could have ever dreamed of? I wish we were man and wife, where you would give me that much pleasure whenever I chose?* But she could never say those words. She didn't have the right, not with what she was planning. He would never forgive her, and she'd rather remember him this way instead of the anger and disappointment he would have when she disappeared.

"We should talk."

"Not tonight." She turned to look out the window and pulled the drapes back with one hand while holding her wrapper closed with the other. It was a splendid night. The moon was crystal clear, lighting up the town and the mine. Her father's mine. Her mine. It was time to let it go.

Cole was right about not firing Huggar, but she wished it had been on her terms instead of Henry and Huggar's. Even if she got pregnant, those two men would do everything in their power to make sure she lost the mine. She wouldn't put it past them to harm the child if it got them what they needed. If she was with child, she had to protect the little one, no matter the cost.

It was time to leave Cole and move forward, even if her heart broke into a thousand pieces.

"Frannie? Look at me."

"I think it's best if you leave." She didn't turn to look at him. If she did, she might surrender. It was better this way.

"I'm not leaving until we talk." His voice was hoarse.

"Not tonight," she said. "We can talk tomorrow. You need to go home before someone realizes you were here."

"But..."

"Please." She was barely holding on to her composure, and if he forced the issue, she'd likely crumble into a puddle on the floor.

"I'll leave, but I'll be back tomorrow. We need to talk, discuss the future."

The sheets rustled behind her as he climbed out of bed. The clang of his belt buckle and the stomping of his feet as he pulled on his boots echoed in her ears.

He stepped behind her, and the heat from his body surrounded her. She shivered, wrapping her arms around her waist, but she still didn't turn to look at him.

Cole touched her shoulder with his hand, but she shrugged away.

"Fran..." He stopped, and a few moments later, her bedroom door opened and shut. The hot tears she'd been holding fell down her icy cheeks unencumbered. She touched her belly and prayed that one day she'd hold Cole's baby in her arms.

If she didn't have that, she had nothing.

Five

July 6, 1865

F rannie sent a note to her lawyer, asking him to stop by that morning. She had asked Carrie to tell Cole she wasn't home if he were to call. The thought of leaving him made her sick, but she had to keep him at arm's length until she figured out her future. If she saw him, she feared she would agree to marry and ruin his future.

Cole might have thought she hadn't known about the plethora of accidents at the mine, but he wasn't her only source. She'd been well aware of what had been happening, even without him telling her and trying to shield her from Henry and Huggar's actions.

Frannie had found dead rats in her study, nasty words scrawled in cow dung on her barn door, broken windows and doors, and several threatening notes. At first, she had thought nothing of them, but as the incidents escalated in intensity, her trepidation had increased.

She hadn't told Cole since he was busy keeping the mine running. The war had kept them in business, but it had been difficult, as men had been scarce. Those who were of fighting age had left, leaving the young and the old, and while they had made do, it had been fraught with issues.

When her lawyer, Mr. Archer, arrived, she left her study and met him and Carrie in the foyer. She greeted him with warmth. "Can you get us a pot of coffee, Carrie?" Mr. Archer confirmed, giving her a slight nod. "And maybe a few of those oatmeal cookies you prepared yesterday?"

Carrie nodded and then disappeared into the kitchen.

"Miss Frannie." Mr. Archer followed her into her father's old study. "What can I do for you?"

"Do you still have the names of those men who wanted to buy my father's mine a few years ago?" She sat behind what used to be her father's desk. She had taken it as her own once he died and his responsibilities had fallen onto her shoulders.

"Ah, um, of course," he said, his voice cracking in disbelief. "Why are you inquiring now?"

"That doesn't matter. Please, contact the most reliable of them and let them know the mine is for sale."

His eyes widened. "You can't sell the mine."

She rose halfway out of her chair, digging her fingers into the hard wood of the desk. "And why not?"

"Because, well... your father's will..."

"My father's will said I had to have a child by the time I was thirty-one. It didn't prohibit me from selling the mines before then."

"But... but that wasn't the intent, I'm sure." Mr. Archer's face had gone pale, sweat gathering across his upper lip. He appeared nervous with his twitching and stuttering.

"Then what was the intent?" She already knew the answer, or at least the answer he'd been pushing on her for months. A part of her wondered if there was something wrong with her father's will. She had a copy of it and had read it word for word. What she never understood was why her father had never told her about the conditions he had placed.

"That..." He swallowed, his Adam's apple bobbing in his throat. "Well, that you were to marry by now, of course." His eyes brightened as though he'd just solved every problem in the world.

She scooted around the desk, pulled a book from the bookcase, and flipped through the pages, although she really wasn't looking at the words. "I'm not getting married, Mr. Archer. We've been through this." She clenched her teeth at his insistence that she find a husband.

"Then you can't sell the mine."

She slammed the book shut. "Of course I can. It's my coal mine, is it not?"

"Well, um, yes, in a manner of speaking, but I mean... you swore that you'd never sell. Why don't you settle down and get married? Then you'll have a child like all proper brides and..."

Were all men this difficult? First, Henry demanding she marry him as though he were the catch of the century. Then Cole insisting she marry him before he gave her a baby to love. Huggar trying to force her to sell to him or he'd continue with his nefarious accidents. And now Mr. Archer acting as though he just had to snap his fingers to get her to do his bidding.

She dropped the book on the desk. "Things have changed. Put the rest of my other properties up for sale as well, but do not, and I mean under any circumstance, consider an offer from Huggar or Henry Davenport."

Mr. Archer's eyes widened, and his fingers danced across his bouncing knee. He had dropped his satchel next to his feet. "I don't understand. Mr. Davenport will inherit the mine, regardless." He plucked a handkerchief from his breast pocket and wiped his forehead.

"Mr. Davenport will never inherit. There's nothing in my father's will that says I can't sell the mine and all of his properties. Since I'm not with child..." However, if anyone were to find out that she had slept with Cole, she would be ruined, and there was no telling what would happen then. For now, she would keep that to herself, and Cole would never divulge their tryst. "And I have no wish to marry to get with said child. The only prudent thing to do to save what I have left is to sell everything before that happens."

"I don't know, Miss Frannie. I'm gonna have to... Well, yes, I'm going to have to consult with the judges here in town." He brightened again.

She slammed her fist onto her father's worn desk, and the papers jumped from the impact of her blow. "You are *not* to consult with anyone, Mr. Archer. I pay you, and there's nothing in Father's will that stops this. Put the properties up for sale."

Seeming to shrink in his seat, he muttered, "All of them?"

"Yes, all of them. Was I not clear?" Heat flushed her cheeks.

"It'll take time to divest of them."

"I don't care how long it takes. Sell them as soon as you can."

"Why the rush?" His eyes were wide.

"Isn't that my business?" She raised a brow at his impertinent question.

"Well, I suppose it is, but I still believe you should think this over and let me consult—"

"I don't have to continue to retain you. There are plenty of other lawyers in town who would love to have my business." Truth be told, she didn't think that was the case. Most were afraid of the Davenport family. The likelihood of men wanting to work with a woman, even if she held the leases on many of their businesses, was unlikely. Many in town were appalled she had carried on with her father's businesses once he passed. Plenty believed she should've married and let a husband take control, but she'd be damned if she'd let any man dictate what she could or couldn't do with her father's money.

He struggled to stand. "Well, I never––"

"You never what?" she demanded.

"You need to learn your place, young lady, or you'll live to regret it." His lip curled into a vicious sneer.

"Are you threatening me, Mr. Archer?" Her lawyer was not on her side.

"No." He straightened his suit jacket and picked up his satchel. "I've been lenient, forgiving since your father and I were friends."

"Friends? I don't believe so." Frannie walked around her father's desk, grazing her fingers against the scarred wood, trying to keep herself from losing her composure. "You were my father's lawyer. I *thought* you were looking after his interests, especially since my father passed, but perhaps I've misjudged you. Mayhap it's time I look for someone who isn't so concerned with Mr. Davenport and his cronies."

"Now, now," he said, shuffling his feet to get out of her way. "There's no need for us to go down that path. I've been looking after your father's interests for years. No need for us to sever that relationship now."

"Then if you're so keen on helping," she drawled, "I suggest you do as I say."

He swallowed hard, smoothing back the remaining strands of gray hair on his head. "Yes, Miss Frannie. I'll be in touch." He turned and scurried out of her study faster than she'd ever seen him move.

She didn't believe he was going to do as she asked. Something was wrong and out of place, and six months before, she would've never believed Mr. Archer was against her. Her gut said Henry Davenport had threatened him. Henry wouldn't want her to sell. If she sold, he wouldn't get a dime, and that likely scared him more than anything else.

Henry had burned through his father's money. His careless spending habits were the talk of the town, and the rumor mill indicated he didn't have much left. His constant and urgent requests for her hand in marriage over the past few weeks only confirmed her suspicions. Time was of the essence. She had to settle her affairs and leave town before anyone was the wiser about what she had done with Cole the night before.

Six

July 12, 1865

Early that morning, she'd stopped at Mr. Archer's home to see if he had had any luck in selling any of her properties when Henry cornered her in Mr. Archer's front parlor. Mr. Archer and his wife had left her there when an emergency had pulled them away, but it had given Henry enough time to say his piace.

Loathing had crawled up her skin when Henry's eyes raked over her, lighting with sinful pleasure.

"You will marry me, Francesca Collins. It's the only way you'll be able to continue to live this way."

"I'll never marry you," Frannie said, cringing when he tried to touch her. "Leave." She pointed toward the door, her chest squeezing, making it difficult to breathe.

Henry's maniacal laughter filled her with dread. "It won't be long before everything belongs to me," he said, ignoring her demand. He sauntered around Mr. Archer's parlor, acting as if he owned the place. "I know about the will. Your pa knew you couldn't lead the mines. No woman can do that, not properly, at least."

"He left it to me," she said, her voice quivering with loathing and fear. She blinked tears away, determined not to let him see her cry.

"No, not really." Henry raised an eyebrow, a cocky smile lined his lips. "He knew you'd never find a man to marry or have a child, so he had a backup plan." Leaning against the fireplace mantel, he dragged his fingers across the glass figurines that rested atop it.

"You weren't part of his will." The thought of him gaining anything her father had worked hard for made her sick.

"Perhaps not directly, but it don't matter now. The law's on my side. If you don't produce a child in three years, it will"--he waved his arms--"all belong to me."

"No, the will only stipulated the mine. Certainly, not my home or..."

He pushed away from the mantle and picked up a ceramic vase, his knuckles turning white. "I'm being generous, Frannie. You can fight this or you can accept it. Either way, you will succumb to my demands."

"Or what?" she drawled, her voice sterner than she felt inside.

"You don't really want to find out. That mental institution on the far side of town don't look highly on women who don't act as they should."

Unease stopped her in her tracks. "I don't belong in a mental institution."

Sweat gathered at her neck and down her back. An inferno of epic proportions had built inside Mr. Archer's parlor. The intense humidity outside made sweat drip off her, but because the parlor faced the sun, it was quite warm inside. However, there was more to it than the heat from outside. A sinister presence had filled the room.

"Maybe, maybe not. A woman's place is in the home. It ain't proper for you to be doing man's work."

"My father--"

"Your father knew it'd be too much for you. That's why he'd

left everything to my pa. Now that my pa is gone, everything will come to me—-just as it should."

"No, you can't have it." She tried to sound braver than she felt, but she feared she failed.

Henry's mouth twisted into an ugly smile. "It won't take much to turn everyone in this town against you. Do you want to be ostracized by everyone you know?"

"That won't happen." Acid rose in her throat.

Henry stepped around the chair and stalked toward her. He was a cougar going after a defenseless rabbit. She was cornered, unable to fight, and he would consume her.

He gripped her chin, holding fast even when she tried to pull away. He leaned close. His hot, acrid breath made her want to gag. He whispered, "Be careful what you say to me or someone might mention they saw a man leave your house late, long past what's proper for an unmarried woman living alone. It won't take much to ruin your reputation." Spittle flew from his mouth, his lips turning into a sneer. "You best get used to the idea of marrying me. You'll be my wife or you'll have nothing but a tarnished reputation, nothing to your name, and living where women who've lost their minds go to live out their lives in utter despair."

She ripped away and scooted from his touch, putting a chair between them. He blocked her from leaving the room and continued to list everything that would happen if she didn't cooperate, his devious smile clear he would stop at nothing to get what he wanted. When she couldn't take it any longer, she took a chance and ran past him, scurrying out like the devil was after her, Henry's laughter following in her wake.

She turned the corner, gasping for air as her heart thundered inside her chest. Henry's threats had done what he had set out to do. She was now more fearful of her future. He would ruin her or have her committed. His best friend was the local judge's son, and the judge had looked the other way at plenty Henry had done over the years. There was no doubt if he wanted to have her committed, the judge would be happy to sign the order.

The women in town barely tolerated her, and once her father passed and she started working at the mine's office, the few who did had stopped talking to her altogether. She had no friends, save for Cole, and she had ruined that friendship by asking him to father her child.

She pushed away from the wall, her eyes furtive as she ran to the bank, the train station, and then home to Carrie, where the support she wanted was there in one way but missing in another.

"Carrie," Frannie hollered, slamming the front door behind her. The windows rattled from the force of her ire. She ripped off her gloves and her hat and dropped them on the entryway table. "Carrie," she cried again. Where was that woman?

"I'm coming, I'm coming." Carried sauntered out of the kitchen and down the hall. The woman had no sense of urgency, and while Frannie appreciated her support and love, there were days when she wondered if Carrie ever got upset or moved quicker than a snail's pace. Carrie had stepped in to raise her when her mother died, but there were times, like today, when her lack of urgency grated on Frannie's last nerve.

"What's the all-fire hurry?" Carrie's cheeks were red from being in the kitchen all morning. From the smells following her, Frannie was sure whatever she had prepared was delicious, but her belly clenched with the thought of trying to eat.

"I have to leave town. I've bought us two train tickets that'll leave this afternoon."

"No, no," Carrie said. "I'm not leaving. This is my home."

"We've talked about this. You know I can't stay, not any longer, and things have taken a turn for the worse. Mr. Davenport knows that I..." She couldn't say the words. She wasn't sure how much Carrie knew about Cole's visit six days past, but considering the side-eyes she gave Frannie every time Cole stopped by and

Frannie refused to see him, Carrie seemed to know far more than what she claimed.

Frannie didn't want to worry Carrie, but she had to leave town. Few choices were left. "He's threatening to ruin me and will have me committed if I don't marry him."

"No one's gonna believe that blowhard," Carrie said. "You've got nothing to worry your pretty little head about."

"I've got everything to worry about," Frannie said, biting her lip. Dread circled like a devil haunting. Never knowing from one minute to the next when it would jump out and try to take her soul. "He said I had until tonight or the orderlies at Lilies for the Mentally Insane would commit me into their institution." As her thoughts jumped from one scenario to the next, she couldn't contain her fear. She had no one to protect her, and while Cole would try, he didn't have the power in town to stop this.

"Now, now, child," Carrie said, placing her hand on Frannie's arm. "He's just trying to scare you."

Frannie spun away, blinking to keep the tears at bay. "It's working, Carrie. I'm scared to death of what Henry will do. Thankfully, Mr. Edwards at the bank gave me most of the cash in my account. The rest, he'd have to get from New York, but he said it would take time. Time I don't have." Mr. Edwards's compassionate smile had almost been her undoing. He had been a close friend of her father's and had always treated her like one of his own. "He's afraid the law will stop him from giving me more."

Carrie's mouth fell open. "Times are a-changing, child. I'm sure if we just sit and talk this through, things won't look so dire."

A lump formed in her throat. Carrie didn't have a mean bone in her body and could never imagine what was happening to Frannie.

"I don't have time. I have to pack and get on that train." Frannie paced back and forth. She likely looked like a crazy woman, and if the judge saw her like this, he'd have her committed in no time. "Mr. Archer visited Mr. Edwards this morning and told him there was concern that I didn't know my mind. He said I wasn't to have any of my funds. Thank the stars Mr. Edwards knows better and gave me everything he could. He said once I'm settled, I'm to send him a letter and he'll try to wire the rest to the closest bank. Without him, I'd be in a world of hurt. I should have enough to last us a while if we're frugal and live simply."

"You're worrying for nothing." Carrie's touch was gentle as she pulled Frannie into her arms, giving her a soothing hug. "No one would believe you need to be put in that horrible place."

Frannie's heart broke. While she had bought two tickets, a part of her knew Carrie wouldn't come with her. Carrie's son depended on her, and she wouldn't be able to make the trip, not at her age and in her condition. Luckily, her father had purchased Carrie a house and left a trust to take care of her in her old age, and Henry shouldn't be able to touch it.

She didn't know where she'd end up, but it'd be far from Pennsylvania. She'd considered going south, but the war had ravaged the region, leaving many without homes or family. Her better choice was to head west. That filled her with trepidation, but she didn't have many options left. It'd be better to go far away where Henry, Huggar, and the judge couldn't find her. She wouldn't let them institutionalize her. She'd have to leave Cole, but she'd always known that.

With any luck, in nine months, she'd have a little one to hold and love. It would be the one thing she could keep of Cole that no one could ever take from her.

Seven

July 15, 1865

"Damnit! Where is she, Carrie?" Cole had been coming by Frannie's every day for the past week. Carrie had an excuse each time why Frannie couldn't see him. He was tired of the excuses. "If you don't get her right now, I'm going to––"

"You're going to do what?" Carrie cocked her hip and raised an eyebrow.

"Carrie, please. I really need to speak with her."

"Not today, you won't," she said.

Cole was done. He pushed past her and strode inside the house. He peered into each room. "Frannie, where are you?"

She wasn't in the parlor, kitchen, or study. He hesitated before heading up the stairs. The last time he'd intruded her sanctuary, they had ended up in bed together. While he wouldn't mind a repeat, it couldn't happen again. There was a slim chance she was with child, and he had to find out if she was. Although it was likely too soon to tell, he needed to see her and make sure she didn't regret what had happened between them.

Knowing it was the only thing she wanted from him stuck in

his craw. It shouldn't, but it did. His emotions had been all over the place since that fateful evening. One minute, he was thinking about her wide eyes, open and innocent but full of pleasure. The next, he realized he could be a father and had potentially broken the promise he had made to himself not to bring a child into this world.

Carrie grabbed his arm just as he stepped onto the first riser. "Mr. Cole, stop. You can't go up there. She isn't here."

Cole took a good look at Carrie. The haunted look in her eyes sent a chill down his spine. Something was wrong, very wrong. He hadn't seen Frannie in ten days. "I don't believe you."

He had to see for himself.

Shrugging off Carrie's hand, he ran up the stairs. He burst into Frannie's bedroom and stood frozen in shock. It had been stripped clean of everything. The only things that remained were the shells of her furniture, looking forlorn and lonely. Her wardrobe stood open and empty, the bedclothes were gone from the bed, and her dressing table was devoid of her frivolities. It was as if she had never lived here.

"I'm sorry. She's gone." Carrie had followed him up the stairs, her eyes wet with tears.

"Where did she go?" He grabbed Carrie and shook her.

Frantic, she tried to pull away. "I don't know. She wouldn't tell me and swore me to secrecy. Told me not to tell anyone she'd left."

"I don't believe you," he said, squeezing her arms.

She whimpered. "Please, Mr. Cole, you're hurting me."

Shocked at his abominable behavior, he let go and stepped back. "I'm sorry. I shouldn't have touched you. Please forgive me."

She rubbed at her arms. Her bottom lip quivering.

He'd overstepped. If she knew more, he'd be hard-pressed to get it from her now.

"Can you tell me anything?" he said, softening his tone.

"No. She didn't want me to have to lie and said it'd be better if I knew nothing."

That sounded exactly like Frannie. She would protect Carrie even at a cost to herself. He was just surprised Frannie had left her behind.

"Why didn't you go with her?"

Carrie lowered her lids, wringing the white apron around her waist. "I'm old, Mr. Cole. There's no way I could make a long trip. Besides, my son needs me."

Cole winced. He had forgotten about Carrie's son. The man had lost a leg in the war and depended solely on Carrie. Frannie wouldn't have been able to ask Carrie to go with her.

He ran a hand against the back of his neck. "I apologize if I hurt you. I'm just concerned."

Perhaps Frannie's lawyer would know where she'd gone. She couldn't have left without telling him. Mr. Archer had a hand in her business dealings. If he could get Mr. Archer to talk, then he'd find the stubborn woman and give her a piece of his mind. Frannie meant the world to him, and he'd never forgive himself if he was the reason she had left town.

Eight

September 1, 1870

"Momma! Momma," Ben yelled as he careened inside, his muddy shoes tracking muck across her clean kitchen floor.

"Slow down, baby," Frannie said as he wrapped his arms around her skirts before reaching into his pocket and pulling out a bullfrog. She had learned not to screech with fear every time he brought a new creature to her, although when he'd brought her a garden snake the last time, her screams had been difficult to hide. "What do you have here?"

"My frog. Look at 'em." He shoved it in her face.

"That's a very nice frog," she said, pulling back. Not enough that he'd notice but enough that she could avoid touching the thing. Frogs gave her the willies. They were ugly, slimy things, but Ben's fascination was enduring, and she hoped it always would be. She encouraged his curiosity. It was one of the many things she loved about her son. "Why don't you go show it to Jacob? I'm sure he'd love to see it."

"Yes, Momma," he said, flying out of the room to go find her friend and handyman, Jacob.

She was lucky Jacob had agreed to stay on to help when they arrived in Virginia City, Montana, four years before.

Jacob had proven invaluable, ensuring her safety on many occasions. He never asked about Ben's father and instead supported every lie she told as though it was the God's honest truth. Sometimes, Jacob said something that made her think he really knew who Ben's father was. He had been the best of friends with Cole.

When she discovered she was pregnant, Frannie had known she had to have a plausible story, and being a widow seemed the easiest and most logical answer. No one knew her, and the last thing she wanted was for Ben to be branded a bastard. Jacob was like a brother, and she was forever beholden to him.

She'd tried to encourage Jacob to leave when she'd gotten settled, but he insisted on staying and hadn't budged in his determination. Frannie sometimes wondered if he was waiting for something, but she could never decide what. She couldn't argue with him though, as he was stubborn as an ox and just as big.

A few minutes later, Jacob bounced into her kitchen, Ben on his shoulders, laughing and carrying the frog. She hoped Jacob would've convinced Ben to let it go, but she should've known better. Jacob wouldn't do anything to disappoint Ben. If Ben wanted the frog, then Ben would keep the frog. Jacob doted on Ben like he was his own son.

"Momma," Ben howled. His movements were excited and full of life.

"You still have your frog?"

"Yup, but Jacob says I have to let it go, 'cause it won't be happy in my room." A frown lined his tiny lips, and his eyes scrunched with irritation.

Inwardly, she sighed with relief. "Oh, he did?"

The last thing she wanted was a bullfrog to be on the loose in the boarding house. She wasn't sure her boarders would be too happy with that. She had a hard enough time keeping them with a rambunctious four-year-old running and playing at all hours of the day. They'd have the same feelings about the critters that Ben was finding and trying to hide in his room. She was glad Jacob had put his foot down on Ben's latest idea.

"Yup."

"So, why do you still have it?" she said, her hands on her hips, trying to look serious but knowing she was failing.

"Well, that's my fault," Jacob said, a piece of hay hanging from between his teeth.

"I shouldn't be surprised. What did you tell him?" She was having a hard time containing her giggles. Trying to be stern, she couldn't help but smile at the picture the two of them made. Jacob would make a good father one day, although he insisted he wasn't about to be one.

"When I told him we needed to let it go, he insisted on showing you his new friend one more time. I couldn't tell him no." Jacob's eyes crinkled with laughter.

She bit her lip to keep from smiling. Ben looked at her as though she'd change her mind if he pouted long enough. "Thank you for bringing him home."

"Momma, you want to hold 'em?" Ben extended his hand. The green and brown frog's long legs dangled from his fingertips, the frog's big round eyes staring at her.

Frannie swallowed and held out her hand, trying not to shake. She could just imagine how slimy and icky it would be, but she couldn't disappoint Ben. His face had lit with enthusiasm, and she wasn't going to ruin his day.

Ben dropped the squirming frog into her palm. Her skin crawled, but to please her son, she ran her fingers across its head, trying to keep a pleasant expression on her face. A second later, Jacob took pity on her and took the frog. It was all she could do not to rush to the pump and scrub her hands raw, but she would wait until he was out of sight.

Placing the frog in his pocket, Jacob swung Ben from around his shoulders and placed him on the ground.

"No, Jacob. I don't wanna get down. Go back." He pointed to Jacob's shoulders.

Jacob shook his head. "Sorry, I've got work to do. Playtime is over for me. I'll come and read you a story before bedtime."

"But what about my frog?" He pouted.

"I'll take care of him for you," Jacob said, squatting to Ben's level.

"I wanna help." Ben put his thumb in his mouth. When he didn't get his way, Ben reverted to his baby antics, although he wasn't much older than a baby in her eyes. In his, he was a big boy, and she needed to remember that when she talked to him.

"I understand, but it's getting late. Your momma is gonna want you to wash up for dinner here soon," Jacob said.

"I'm not hungry," Ben mumbled, spittle running down his chin.

Jacob smiled, ruffling his hair. "I'm not too sure about that. You're always hungry. Now, you mind your momma, all right?"

"Yes, sir."

"I better get outside. Do you need anything?" Jacob raised his eyes to hers.

"No," Frannie said. "Dinner will be ready soon. Are you joining us tonight, or should I save a plate for you?"

"Not tonight, Fran. I've got plenty to do in the barn before it gets dark, but I'd appreciate you making me up one. I'll come inside when I'm done."

"All right, if that's what you want."

Jacob typically stayed away from the house at dinnertime, not wanting to spend time with the boarders who rented rooms in the large three-story house she'd purchased when they arrived. "I'll keep it in the warming oven. You can come for it when you're ready."

He nodded, then turned his gaze toward her son. "Now, Ben, I'm gonna take your frog and let him go into the pond."

"What if he gets hurt?" Ben asked, his eyes soulful as he considered the possibilities.

"We can't protect all God's creatures, young man. You know that. We've had that discussion plenty of times, but I know one thing for certain."

"What's that?" Ben asked, his brown eyes focused on Jacob as if he were his entire world. Ben wanted a father, and it broke Frannie's heart that she couldn't give him that. Jacob was the next best thing, and she appreciated Jacob for filling in where Ben needed it.

"That the frog'll be much happier in the pond where he can jump, play, and eat all the little bugs to his heart's content."

"I can give him bugs here," Ben said.

"Maybe, but do you think he'll be happy being locked up?"

"Yes!"

Jacob shook his head. "Now, young man, you know better than that."

"Oh, all right," Ben said, irritated with Jacob, but at least he agreed.

Frannie hid a smile behind her hand, covering it before Ben caught sight of it, although she wasn't quick enough to hide it from Jacob.

"Can I say goodbye?" Ben asked.

"Of course," Jacob said, pulling the frog from his pocket.

Ben ran his finger across the frog's head and then gave it a big, smacking kiss. Frannie cringed, but she was relieved he wasn't giving Jacob any lip about releasing the frog back into the pond.

Jacob held the frog up to Frannie and grinned. "Wanna say goodbye, Fran?"

She glared at him. "No, thank you."

"Well, if'n you're sure. I'll see myself out." He shoved the frog back into his pocket and walked out the door, whistling a merry tune as the door swung closed behind him.

Smiling to herself, Frannie turned back to Ben. "Go wash your hands, young man." Looking at the dirt streaks on his face and shirt, she shook her head. "You should put on a clean shirt, and why don't you run a wet rag across those cheeks? Dinner'll be ready soon."

"Ah, Momma, do I have to?"

She eyed him and didn't say a word. He sighed and scurried out of the room, his footsteps heavy as he ran up the stairs.

Ben was a charmer, and his personality was engaging. He reminded her too much of his father and would no doubt break a few hearts as he got older, just as his father had done to hers.

Cole coughed as he grasped the edge of the stagecoach door and stepped down the rickety steps. His gaze roamed the booming gold rush town. Dirt and dust flew as a warm wind whipped through the streets. He patted his breast coat pocket, the letter from Jacob resting inside.

He'd received the letter months before and read it over and over. The edges were curled and words smudged from the hundreds of times he'd read it while he decided if he should follow. It'd been the first time in four years he had heard from Jacob. He had been shocked but pleasantly surprised to receive the news.

Cole had wondered what had happened to him after he left Pennsylvania. In his letter, Jacob had told him about the gold in this part of the country and how Cole would be a fool not to try his hand at finding some. Cole wasn't sure he hadn't missed the peak of the gold rush and had almost ignored the summons, considering he'd continued to hold out hope Frannie would return. But after months of thinking about the letter, he'd finally decided he was a fool to stay in Pennsylvania waiting for a woman who had run without telling him where she was going. No one had heard from her in the five years she'd been gone. It'd be best for him to forget about her, but he couldn't, no matter how hard he tried.

Unfortunately, it'd taken Frannie leaving for him to realize what had stood in front of him. He'd never find anyone as special, and he would regret his actions for the rest of his life. Coming to Virginia City, Montana, could help him start anew, and with any luck, he'd be too busy to think about her.

Stepping away from the stagecoach and the passengers following him, he moved to the wooden walkway a few feet away. Jacob hadn't said where Cole could find him, but he couldn't imagine Virginia City was so big that someone didn't know the man. Jacob stood out in a crowd, and there were few men like him.

"Mister," the stagecoach driver yelled, "is this your bag?"

Cole raised his eyes and found the man kneeling across the luggage rack, throwing bags to each of the passengers. Cole nodded and raised his hands to receive his carpetbag. The driver tossed it, and the bag hit him hard in the chest. He grunted under the weight. While he didn't have much, he had enough to make him stumble.

Pushing back his hat, he thanked the driver and moved out of the way of the other flying bags. The driver must've had a schedule to keep. Cole looked both ways before deciding to head north. It was getting late, and he needed to find nightly accommodations. With any luck, a hotel or a boarding house would have a room for him.

It had been weeks since he'd left Pennsylvania. The trip out West had been eventful as well as beautiful. While things were settling after the war, there were still hurt feelings and animosity toward those who'd lost. It'd be a pleasant change to get away from the anger and start somewhere new, where men were looking for a new life and were open to grabbing the abundant opportunities.

While he'd miss working at the mine, it hadn't been the same since Henry Davenport took possession. Cole didn't understand what had happened and had tried to fight it, but Henry had had the law on his side and had Frank's last will and testament to back up his claims. When Frannie disappeared, Henry had swooped in and had taken over.

Luckily, Henry had kept him on, but Cole had wondered many times over the years if that had been a blessing or a curse. The mine conditions had deteriorated, and the coal mine produced less and less. Cole had saved every penny he earned and had a nice nest egg saved, but it wouldn't last long if he didn't find work or some gold. He wasn't looking to strike it rich, but just enough to buy himself a spread with horses and a few heads of cattle. Cole hadn't thought much about owning a ranch, but it seemed like a good way to make a living. He didn't know much about ranching, but he was willing to learn. A strong back and a determination to make something of himself was all he needed. He was still young and had plenty of hard work left in him.

A few minutes later, he walked inside the mercantile and found it bustling. The storekeeper and presumedly his wife stood behind the counter helping the customers as they made their purchases. Swift and efficient, they tended to each person and their needs as money exchanged hands and happy people left the building when they were finished.

The store was stuffed full of goods. Bags of flour, rice, and sugar rested against the wall. Barrels held crisp red and green apples. Tables held bolts of fabric, and ready-made clothing hung on racks. Cooking implements, farming supplies, ribbons, thread, lanterns, clocks, kerosene, blankets, threshers, shovels, pick-axes, and numerous other items that any rancher, farmer, or miner could need. It was almost more expansive than what he'd find back East. The storekeeper must have a generous and competent supplier.

Cole wandered around, looking at the various goods and making a mental checklist of what he might need once he found a permanent place to put down roots. For now, he'd depend on what a boarding house or hotel could offer. Grabbing a loaf of fresh bread, he lifted it to his nose and inhaled. It was warm, and his mouth watered. He was starving, and maybe the proprietor of the hotel or boarding house would provide him with a crock of butter and some preserves. He wouldn't mind some cheese and salt pork, but what was available was more than he could eat. He had no place to store anything, so best to live with just the loaf of bread. It would be tasty, regardless, and he'd eat it before it could go bad.

Standing in the long line, he observed those in front of him. There was nothing more enjoyable than watching the behavior of others, and while he rarely had the time to people-watch, when he did, it was something he appreciated.

He sometimes wondered what it was like to be a storekeeper. They knew the most about people in town, as it was a hotbed of gossip and general information. Cole figured the storekeeper was the place to start in helping direct him to a place to stay for the night. He'd also inquire if they knew Jacob and where he might find him.

A few minutes later, he reached the long wooden counter. A family of five had just finished purchasing several goods and a few pieces of candy for the children. He'd chuckled under his breath, seeing the children stomp their feet in frustration when their pa didn't buy them a whole jar full of black licorice. He had been firm yet gentle in his love that one piece was more than enough for each of them.

"What can I get for you, mister?" The storekeeper was looking a bit harried after the large family left. They'd been demanding, but he had handled it well and with a respect that was missing back East. "You must be new here." He eyed Cole's bag.

"I am. You've got a nice little town here." Cole placed the loaf of bread on the counter and pulled out a few coins to pay for it.

The storekeeper smiled, took the coins, then tightened the

once-white apron around his waist. "It's a fair place. Do you want me to wrap the bread?"

"Yes, please. I'm Cole Seymour." He placed his bag on the counter and opened it so he could put the bread inside. Although, as hungry as he was, he'd rather tear a chunk off and eat it now, but he had some manners left inside of him.

"John Mercury," the storekeeper said. "Nice to meet you."

Cole nodded. "I don't want to hold up the line, but I was wondering if you could tell me if there's a hotel or boarding house in town where I can get a room?"

John leaned back against the shelves behind him after looking to see if anyone was waiting behind Cole. Glancing over his shoulder, Cole realized he was alone for the moment, which was likely why the storekeeper seemed more relaxed.

"No line behind ya, thank the lord." He chuckled. "It's been right busy in here this afternoon. I'm glad for the break."

"I'm sure, although being busy is a good problem to have, I'd imagine."

Tugging at his bright red suspenders, John said, "Yep, it is, though I don't mind a break here and there to catch my breath." He grinned a toothy smile. "Now, to answer your question. We have a couple of boarding houses in town. I wouldn't recommend the hotel such as it is, not for a man such as yourself." He eyed Cole carefully.

Cole wasn't sure if that was a good thing or not, but there was no cause to disagree with the man. "Do you know if any of them have rooms available?"

"Not at Mrs. Clemson's. She's always full up and rarely has a room open, but Mrs. Black likely has some. She can't keep it full on account of that young'un she has running around, screaming, and playing at all hours of the day and night. Mrs. Black should take the child to task, but..." John pushed away from the shelves. "I shouldn't be going on like that, Mr. Seymour. She's a gracious lady and all, but raising her son alone has got to be hard on anyone."

"Oh, is she a widow?"

"Yep. Sounds as though he made it through the war, but he caught influenza once he got home. A shame, really. So many men died at the hands of others, and to have him come home and die from a dreaded disease just don't seem right."

"No, it doesn't," Cole said. Plenty of women had lost their husbands to the war, disease, and unfortunate accidents. It was time for death to end for everyone. He was tired of it himself.

"So, if you don't mind a rambunctious young'un runnin' around, you'll likely get a room there. She needs the help, truth be told."

"Oh?" Cole didn't want to be nosy, but he couldn't help but be curious about the woman.

"She has a man who sees to the horses and such. Rumor has it he's itching to leave but doesn't want to leave her alone without someone else stepping up."

"Is he family?"

"Nah, just someone she met on the stagecoach, I believe. He's a brother to her, or at least that's what they claim." John raised an eyebrow and wiggled it. "I, myself, wonder if the man wouldn't want to have more, but she ain't inclined to seek anything more from him or from any other man in town." He put his hands against the counter and shifted forward. "Personally, I believe she's being a mite picky. She needs a husband but turns away every man who looks her way. A bit high in the instep if you ask me, but I guess she wants to raise that boy alone."

Cole hid his smile. John was a gold mine of town gossip, which was good when you were new and needed information but not so good if you wanted to keep your secrets to yourself. Cole would have to watch his step around the man if he stayed in town.

"Thank ya kindly for the information," Cole said. "But it's getting late. I should see if she has a room available before I have no place to stay for the night." He chuckled. "Not that I don't mind roughing it, but as you can see, I have little with me. I'll send for the rest of my belongings once I know where I can put down some roots."

John scratched his chin. "You here to look for gold?"

"Not sure yet. I've thought about owning a ranch, but that takes cash, so I'll see what this part of the country has to offer."

John nodded. "For now, I suggest lookin' to stay with Mrs. Black. If she has nothing available, there are plenty of saloons where you can rent a room if you're so inclined." He waggled his eyebrow.

Cole shook his head. "Nah, I'd rather not, so I best be getting to her place. Can you point me in the right direction?"

"Sure thing, Mr. Seymour." He stepped from out behind the counter and led Cole outside.

"Call me Cole," he said.

"Cole." John smiled and pointed to the right. "Go past the jailhouse, hang a left, and you'll see it at the end of the stretch of road. You can't miss it. It's a big ole three-story monstrosity that's seen better days. She and that man of hers fixed it up as best they could, but it could use a good coat of paint. It has dark green shutters and a wide wraparound porch."

"Thank you kindly, Mr. Mercury."

"No need for formalities out here. Call me John. I'm sure we'll see each other again."

Cole doffed his hat and stepped away from the doors and just in time, too. A whole gaggle of children had rushed inside and were running around the stacks of dry goods, screeching in their haste to get to the jars of gumdrops, licorice, and peppermint sticks. Cole was glad he wasn't the one to corral those young'uns, but he realized he'd failed to ask about Jacob. He would come back in the morning. It was best to get a place for the night. If Jacob was here, he'd find him soon enough.

Nine

Frannie screeched. The mop flew from her hands and crashed to the floor. Few people knocked on her front door this late in the afternoon. She'd been mopping the hallway floors, singing a ditty in her head, when the sharp knocks startled her. She almost kicked over the bucket of dirty water and crashed into the wall in trying to avoid it. Thankfully, she stopped herself before she'd dirtied the clean floors.

Pushing back stray hairs that had fallen from her bun, she picked up the mop, rested it against the wall, and went to answer the door when whoever was outside knocked loudly again. They were surely impatient.

"I'm coming, I'm coming," she muttered. She couldn't imagine it was anyone wanting to rent a room. As hard as she tried, it was difficult to convince people to stay for long periods of time. Keeping Ben quiet was next to impossible, and she didn't enjoy stifling his enthusiasm. He was a young boy and deserved to run and play as much as he'd like. She wouldn't be like some of her neighbors, who believed children should be seen but not heard. That was an old adage that didn't belong, not anymore. He had energy and curiosity, and she wanted to encourage it.

Taking a deep breath and schooling her expression so she didn't look as irritated as she felt, she reached for the door and pulled it open, a bright smile on her face.

"Good afternoon," she said.

"Mrs. Black."

Frannie cringed. It was her neighbor, Mrs. Greer. She was an unpleasant woman who consistently complained about Ben, the men who stayed in her boarding house, and even Jacob, claiming he was a lout who wasn't fit to be around proper society folks. Every time she visited, Frannie had to find the strength not to slap the woman with her critical attitude and endless unkind words.

"Mrs. Greer, how nice to see you." Frannie swallowed back the lie. It wasn't nice to see the tall, thin woman with her beady eyes, hawklike appearance, and black hair slicked tight. It was a wonder her scalp didn't cry from the strain. "Why don't you come in and sit a spell?"

"No, thank you," Mrs. Greer said, her hands fisted at her hips, her cheeks bright red, and an unpleasant scowl across her lips. "I am *not* here for a social call."

Frannie didn't know what had happened, but she was sure Mrs. Greer thought it was of the utmost importance. If Frannie didn't do as she bid, it would turn the molehill into a mountain of epic proportions.

"What can I do for you, Mrs. Greer?"

She hmphed, the scowl on her face growing even more stern with each passing second. It was as though steam were rolling out of the woman's ears. Whatever had happened had angered her more than ever. Frannie wasn't sure she wanted to have this conversation, but she knew Mrs. Greer would have to get it off her chest, otherwise she'd make a spectacle of Frannie in some other fashion. She was known to blast her displeasure in a crowd full of people. The townsfolk did care to gossip, so any bit of drama was delicious candy to someone's lips.

Frannie kept quiet, waiting for Mrs. Greer to continue.

"That... that child of yours," she sputtered.

Frannie fingered the collar of her shirt. Mrs. Greer had nothing but horrible things to say about her son, especially since Ben had no visible father. Frannie was afraid Mrs. Greer didn't believe her story of being a widow and wouldn't be surprised if she'd find someone from Pennsylvania to substantiate her opinion.

"His behavior is unacceptable. I won't stand for this much longer."

"He's just a little boy—" Frannie's voice cracked.

Mrs. Greer held up her hand and waved it belligerently in her face. "He has no manners, does not listen to his elders, and needs to be disciplined. I've had enough of him. If you don't do something about him, I will."

The fine hair on the back of Frannie's neck stood straight. "He's four years old, Mrs. Greer. He's barely out of toddler strings. You'll do nothing to my child."

"How dare you speak to me like that," she huffed. "You're just as bad as your son."

"I may be," Frannie said, "but he's mine, and I'll raise him as I see fit."

"Perhaps if you had a man who could control him, then he'd be better behaved."

Frannie bristled at Mrs. Greer's words, and it took everything in her not to wrap her fingers around the woman's neck. "I don't need a man to control my child."

Mrs. Greer pointed her finger at Frannie's chest. "You need a man all right. It isn't proper for you to be running this place alone and letting that unruly child continue to be unsupervised."

"My husband passed away, Mrs. Greer, and I—"

"That is what you say, but how are we to know any different? Any proper woman would have gone home to her family, into her pa's care, or found herself a man to take care of her."

Sighing, Frannie knew the woman wouldn't leave her be until she said everything she needed to say. Frannie would just have to nudge her along and pray she didn't hurl insults at the woman before she was done. Mrs. Greer had already stopped plenty of men from taking a room at her boarding house, and Frannie really couldn't afford for her to continue to bad-mouth her to their neighbors and anyone who came to town. She wasn't poor, but the banker, Mr. Edwards, had been prevented from sending her the rest of her father's money, so what she had left had to last. It had been far more expensive to have the boarding house than she'd imagined.

"What did he do now?" Frannie really didn't want to hear what misdeed Ben had gotten himself into. He never did anything unforgivable, but Mrs. Greer would prefer if Ben stayed inside the house and not be outside playing like the little boy he was.

Sneering, the woman was pleased as punch that Frannie appeared to have capitulated. For the next ten minutes, Mrs. Greer told her in excruciating detail how horrible her son was. Ben had apparently been playing with a bunch of boys behind Mrs. Greer's home. She had a pond that many of the boys in town loved to fish in. As long as they played far away from her back porch and kept their noise level down, she ignored the children. Today, the boys had broken both rules and played on the edge closest to her flower garden.

While playing, the boys got into a tussle and wreaked havoc on her flowers. They tore through four of her most prized rose bushes and ruined several other flower beds and full green bushes. Mud had been slung, rocks thrown, and the boys had left things in disarray.

When Mrs. Greer confronted the boys, they'd run off except for Ben, who she snatched by the scruff of his neck. Frannie's eyes widened and a red-hot haze grew inside of her when Mrs. Greer told her that, but she didn't give Frannie a chance to say a word. Instead, she went on and on about how Ben had swung his fists at her, yelling and screaming to let go. He had kicked her in the shin, and Mrs. Greer was happy to lift her skirts, pointing to the skin that had been bruised.

"What are you going to do to control that heathen of yours, Mrs. Black?"

Frannie still wasn't used to being called Mrs. Black, so it took her a moment to realize Mrs. Greer was speaking to her. She took a breath. "I'll speak with him once he comes home, Mrs. Greer."

"Is that all?" she spat out.

Frannie pulled her arms behind her back and clutched her fingers together, trying to keep her composure. "What more would you like me to do? He's only four. He was likely following the lead of the older boys."

"That is precisely my point. He should not be acting like that, hitting and kicking at his elder. If you don't get ahold of him now, he will most definitely turn into a worthless—"

"I'll stop you right there. You come to my home, speaking to me with disrespect. I listened to you, but now you'll listen to me." Frannie stepped past the threshold of her front door, her back straight.

Mrs. Greer's eyes widened, her mouth falling open, before she retreated. "Why, you—"

"I've been patient, but I'm done. You said your piece. You can leave now." Frannie pointed past the insolent woman's shoulder.

"Why, I've never met anyone so impertinent in all my years. I can see where your son gets his unruliness from. Mark my words, you'll regret not taking him in hand when he grows up and becomes a blight on society." Mrs. Greer spun around and marched down the steps.

Frannie would regret saying what she had, but she could only take so much. Mrs. Greer was mean and spiteful and had been ever since she arrived in Virginia City without a husband and pregnant. She had always assumed the worst about Frannie and believed she had lied about Ben's father. The side glances she received in church and on the street were disconcerting.

Hoping that Ben wouldn't have to live with the stigma of being a bastard, she was afraid that Mrs. Greer and those who believed her would always hold it against her for not being married. In their eyes, she was a fallen woman, and although technically they were right, it didn't serve her or her son well for them to believe that.

"Whoa, young man. Where do you think you're going in such a hurry?" Cole grabbed the little boy who had slammed into his knees. Streaks of dirty tears lined his plump cheeks. His dark brown hair stood high on one side and was matted with something unidentifiable on the other. He'd been in a recent skirmish with a long, ragged gash in his shirt sleeve and a large rip at his knee.

The boy gazed at him in fear, his hands shaking. Whatever had happened to the boy must've been traumatic, and his heart tugged. The boy's ma and pa would be horrified to see him in this state. Cole had always believed he wouldn't have children, but seeing this little one made him regret his reaction to Frannie and how he had treated her. But it was too late. He had burned that bridge, and there was no recovery from that.

Squatting to the boy's level, he looked him in the eye, hoping he didn't scare him. "What's your name, son?"

Sniffling back tears, the boy wiped at his face, smearing more dirt across his cheek. He raised a thumb to put in his mouth but then stopped. He looked at it, looked at Cole, and then shoved his hand behind his back. Cole had to smother a snicker at the boy's desire to suck his thumb, conflicting with his determination to be a big boy. The boy couldn't be more than four or five.

"Benjamin, but Momma says I can go by Ben 'cause it sounds right smart and 'cause Benjamin is a mouthful." He brightened at that.

"I'd have to agree, Ben," Cole said. "Can I call you Ben?"

Ben tilted his head to the side, narrowing his eyes. "What else would you call me?"

Cole bent his head to hide his smile. He removed it before lifting his head. "You're right. Ben is your name, and so Ben is what I'll call you."

"Good," Ben said. "What's your name, mister?"

He tipped his hat back. "Cole."

"Cole. I like that." His brown eyes had cleared of tears, and a cute smile lifted his cheeks.

"I'm glad you do. Now, do you want to tell me what's bothering you?"

The smile that lined Ben's lips dropped into a frown. "Not really." He avoided looking at Cole, shuffling his feet in the dirt.

"Why not?"

"'Cause..." Ben kicked at a pile of rocks. It scattered, the pebbles rolling this way and that.

"Did something dangerous happen?" Cole asked, nodding toward the rip in Ben's sleeve.

Ben's eyes widened, and he shook his head. The boy was terrified, and Cole didn't want to scare him further.

Taking a breath, Cole released the handle of his bag and scratched behind his ear. "Do you know the difference between right and wrong?"

Ben slowly nodded.

"Did your ma or pa teach you to tell the truth?"

"I don't have a pa." His eyes were sad with that pronouncement.

Cole placed a hand on the boy's shoulder and squeezed gently. "I'm sorry to hear that. It's mighty hard not having a pa, isn't it?"

"Yes," he said, the word slowly emerging from his little mouth. "My momma says he's in heaven looking over me, but I wish he was here instead. The other boys each have a pa, so why can't I?"

"That's a good question, Ben. Sometimes, things happen that

we cannot stop. I'm sure your ma does her best and loves you something fierce if I were to hazard a guess."

Ben nodded. "She does. She tells me every night how much she loves me."

Ben smiled. "She sounds like the perfect momma."

"She is." Ben's eyes shone with a happiness that only the love of a good mother would give a boy. Cole wished his ma could have given him that, but now wasn't the time to ruminate over his ma not having the capacity to love her family like Cole had wished.

As Cole shifted, his knees creaked under him. "Do you want to tell me what happened?

"No. Nothing happened." His forehead scrunched.

"Should you tell your momma what happened?"

"No. She'd be mad if she knew." Ben twisted his hands, nervous energy seeming to ooze out of him.

Cole had no doubt this little boy likely kept his mother on her toes. "So, something did happen."

Ben shook his head so fast that if it hadn't been attached, it'd likely fly off with the force of his denial.

"Should we go to your momma and ask her about it?"

"No," Ben said, tears filling his eyes. "She'd be sad if she knew."

"Did you do something wrong?"

"No. Not me, but... Mrs. Greer, she..." Ben gulped, tears running down his cheeks before he hiccupped and sobs tore from his throat.

"Ah, little man." Cole's heart tore. This little boy was hurting, and he needed to get him home to his ma as soon as possible. "Everything's gonna be all right."

"No, it won't," Ben mumbled, sniffling back the snot running from his nose.

Cole pulled out a handkerchief and wiped the boy's face. Ben mumbled something, but he didn't stop Cole from cleaning him, likely cause his ma had done it for him before.

"Momma's gonna be so mad," Ben said when Cole lifted the handkerchief away.

Cole quirked an eyebrow. "At you?"

"No." Ben frowned. "She's gonna be mad at Mrs. Greer, and it's all my fault."

"I'm sure it's not as rotten as you think. Why don't we go find your momma and talk it out?"

"I don't wanna." He grabbed the front of his shirt, his little fingers almost ripping the fabric from his tiny chest.

"What are you going to do, then?"

Ben avoided Cole's gaze. "I dunno."

"We should talk to your momma." Cole didn't want to push the little boy too far, but he couldn't leave him out there.

"No, I won't." Ben stomped his foot.

The young boy was obstinate. Cole wondered what had happened to his pa. "It's getting late. Your momma is likely worried sick that you haven't come home for dinner. How about I take you to her? Your momma sounds like a smart woman."

"She is." Ben brightened. "You wanna meet her?"

"I'd like that. Are we going to tell her what happened?" Cole held up his hand to stop the boy from talking. "I'm thinking that since she is such a smart woman..."

"She is." Ben jumped with enthusiasm.

Cole removed his hat to wipe the sweat that had gathered across his brow. The hot sun would set soon, but he wasn't too sure it'd be cool enough to suit him. "Since you've told me how smart she is, I'm thinking she's going to understand whatever happened and will be more upset if you don't and she finds out from someone else."

"Oh, all right." He frowned at Cole and flicked at one shirt button. "I don't wanna, though."

"I know, son, but it's always best to get the hard things over with right quick. Then you can go back to playing and being happy, don't ya think?" Cole stood to his full height, and Ben stared at him with wonder in his eyes.

"You're tall."

Cole laughed. "I suppose I am." He picked up his bag. "Where to, young man?"

Ben grabbed Cole's hand. "This way." He pulled Cole down the road the same way he'd been going when the boy ran into him. "Momma's gonna like you."

Ben had picked up speed and was jogging, pulling Cole with him. Before long, they had arrived at a three-story home with dark green shutters. It appeared Ben was the boy the storekeeper, John, was telling him about. If he was the rambunctious child everyone was concerned about, then he'd find the boarding house a welcome place to stay. With any luck, John would be right, and there'd be a room for him to sleep in, as he wouldn't mind spending more time with the sweet little boy who held his hand.

Ten

Ben dragged Cole around to the back of the house instead of to the front door, where a large red barn stood.

"Where are we going, Ben?"

"To the barn."

"Is your ma inside there?"

Ben stopped and looked up at Cole, his expression confused. "No, she thinks it smells." He wiggled his nose. "Momma don't come out here unless she's looking for Jacob."

Cole squeezed Ben's hand, forgetting he was a child.

"Ow!" Ben pulled his hand from Cole's and shook it. "That hurt. Why'd you do that, Cole?"

"I'm sorry. I was just startled when you mentioned Jacob."

"Why?" He leaned his head back.

"I came to Virginia City looking for an old friend of mine. His name was Jacob. I wonder if it's the same man."

Ben grinned, his lips opening and revealing a missing front tooth that Cole hadn't noticed before. The young boy was quite endearing. If he'd ever agreed to have a son, one like Ben would be a delight.

"Maybe he's your friend." Ben grabbed his hand again and pulled him forward. "Let's go see."

Cole shook his head and laughed. Ben was charming, and his enthusiasm was contagious. Cole would be happy if it was the same man, but the likelihood was slim. The town had thousands of people, and the name Jacob was a common enough one. It would be a coincidence, and a lucky one at that, if it was his longtime friend.

They reached the barn doors, and Ben dropped Cole's hand. He reached to pull the doors open, his small body straining. Cole went to help, but Ben pushed his hand away.

"I can do it." His lips pursed tight as he put all his weight behind him, trying without success to get it open. Ben dropped his hands. "Oh, for hell's sake." Ben slapped his hand over his mouth and reddened when he caught the censure in Cole's eyes.

Cole shook his head. "I don't know what your momma might think, but I'm sure she wouldn't be happy with what you just said."

Ben slapped his hands against his thighs. "Oh, all right, but Momma ain't close by so..."

Cole ruffled Ben's hair. "She might not be near, but I'm sure she's raising you to be a gentleman."

"That's what she says," he muttered. "You sound like her."

"Is that a bad thing?"

"Nah, I don't think so." He pointed to the door. "Let's go find Jacob."

Cole grabbed the barn door and pulled it open. While it had been hard for Ben, it took little effort for Cole to move it. Once the door opened, Ben rushed inside, yelling for Jacob.

The barn was dark with the sun setting in the distance, and it took a moment for Cole's eyes to adjust, but Ben didn't have the same problem. Of course, he'd likely gone into the barn plenty of times, so he knew his way around.

"Jacob," Ben hollered. "Where are you?"

Grunts, groans, and a horse neighing was all Cole heard. Ben had startled the horses, and Cole was sure his friend Jacob wouldn't appreciate the intrusion, especially if he was trying to get the horses and other animals settled for the night.

"What in all that's holy are you doing, young'un?" a man yelled. "You know better than to come in here screeching like that. Getting the horses riled up and just when I'd gotten 'em settled."

"Sorry, Jacob," Ben said, his voice contrite. "I didn't mean to."

Jacob laughed, and the sound was reminiscent of Cole's old friend. Could it be as easy as this? Had he stumbled upon his friend all because of the young boy?

A moment later, Ben came into view, holding a man's hand. He stepped into the waning light.

"Is that you, Cole Seymour?" Jacob dropped Ben's hand, strode toward Cole, and pulled him into his massive arms. The man had gotten bigger in the past few years. Cole thought Jacob would've stopped growing by now. His shoulders were broader, and his face was more defined. He was built like a bear, but a friendly one at that.

Jacob slapped Cole's back, and tears of joy threatened to spill from Cole's eyes. He hadn't expected to find Jacob quickly, and it was a welcome surprise. Until this moment, he hadn't realized how much he had missed him.

Pulling away, Cole grinned. "You sure are a sight for sore eyes, Jacob."

"It's about time you got here. When you didn't answer my letter, I thought for sure you'd moved on and never received it."

"Sorry about that. I read it so many times, it's near worn to pieces."

Jacob grinned. "Didn't realize I held such a dear place in your heart."

Cole chuckled, one that came from deep within his chest. He hadn't laughed that hard in some time. "Oh, you. I'd forgotten what a jokester you were."

"Who says I was joking?" Jacob had a serious expression on his face, but his eyes twinkled in mirth. "It sure is good to see you. How'd you find me?"

Ben was swiveling his head back and forth between the two of them, watching the byplay. Cole placed his hand on Ben's head. "This little one found me and said he had a good friend named Jacob. Didn't expect it to be you, but I'm sure glad it is."

"What has this little scamp been up to?" Jacob asked.

"Nothin'," Ben said, suddenly backing away.

"I don't think so, young man," Jacob said, gently grabbing Ben by the arm and pulling him to a stop. "Your shirt's torn, and you've got a big ole hole in your pants. I know for certain your ma wouldn't have sent you outside looking like this."

"I was just playin'," Ben mumbled, not looking at either of them.

Jacob looked at Cole and lifted a brow. It wasn't Cole's place to tell him what had happened. He nodded toward Ben and communicated with his eyes that Jacob needed to ask the little boy.

Kneeling in front of Ben, Jacob put a finger under his chin and lifted it, forcing the boy to look at him. "Something happened. I've got two eyes and the caginess of a bear to know you're hiding something."

Ben shook his head, keeping his eyes averted. His little body shook, and tears leaked from his eyes.

"Hey," Jacob said, "you know you've got nothing to fear from me."

Ben launched himself into Jacob's arms, great big sobs coming from his chest. Jacob stood and held Ben's little body close, letting the boy cry. "What in the world?"

Cole couldn't let this continue. "I don't know what happened, but he's quite scared to tell his ma. He says his ma's going to be mad at a Mrs. Greer and that whatever happened is his fault. I think he's afraid she's gonna be spittin' mad."

"Ah, Ben, you know your ma ain't like that. She won't lay a

finger on your head." Jacob rubbed Ben's back in comforting circles until Ben's shoulders stopped shaking.

Ben sniffled and pulled his head from Jacob's shoulder. "I know she won't. She's just gonna be angry at Mrs. Greer. I don't want her to be. Mrs. Greer's mean, but she'll be meaner to Momma. I heard Momma tell you just the other day that Mrs. Greer would ruin her and have her cast out into the outer darkness if she had half the chance. I don't want her to do that to Momma, and now she's gonna 'cause of me."

Jacob's face crinkled with concern, but he patted Ben's back. "Don't you worry about Mrs. Greer. Your momma's made of sturdy stuff. There's nothing Mrs. Greer can do that'd hurt your momma. Now, why don't we go to the well, wash that face of yours, tuck in your shirt, and go face her? She's been worried sick when you didn't show up to dinner on time. I was just about to go look for you when you ran hollering into the barn."

Ben shook his head. "I don't wanna. Can I stay out here with you?"

"Benjamin, you know better than that. It's better to face your problems instead of hiding. You'll feel much better once you talk to her."

"No, I won't," he mumbled into Jacob's chest.

Jacob grinned and waved for Cole to follow. A few minutes later, they had cleaned Ben at the well as best they could, but they couldn't hide the torn shirt and pants. Ben would have to face his momma and provide an explanation, even if he had no desire to. After a stern look from Jacob and a gentle talking to about being the man of the house, Ben straightened his shoulders and marched toward the porch, glancing over not once but twice to make sure both Jacob and Cole were following him.

Ben stopped, shrugged his slight frame as though he was preparing for battle, opened the back door, and went inside the house. Cole followed, but Jacob held out his hand and stopped him.

"Cole, I better tell you something before you go inside."

He stopped and caught the look of concern in Jacob's eyes. "Is everything all right?"

"Yes, but--"

A woman's frantic hollering cut off Jacob's words. Jacob brushed past Cole and ran inside the house. Cole wondered what was going on but figured it wasn't his place. He placed his bag on a table sitting just outside the door and settled into a rocking chair. The sun had fully disappeared behind the mountains while they had dealt with Ben's calamity. A breeze blew through the air, lifting the collar of his chambray shirt.

Jacob had told him there were plenty of rooms available in the boarding house, but Cole would wait until Ben had talked with his mother before announcing himself and asking for a room. With any luck, the woman would rent him one after the arrival of her frightened little boy. He hoped the woman was sympathetic, but he likely shouldn't worry. Considering how sweet the boy was, he was sure his mother was just as sweet.

Frannie paced back and forth in the kitchen. She had finished cleaning the dining room after the few boarders finished dinner, and her worry was growing with each second. After Mrs. Greer left, she had found Jacob and asked if he had seen Ben. He hadn't but told her he would look for the boy. He didn't think she had any cause to worry, but after Mrs. Greer's tirade, she wasn't so sure.

Mrs. Greer had likely put the fear of God into her little boy, and it worried her heart to know she had. Ben wasn't afraid of her, but something had scared him. He should have been home by now, and Frannie feared he had either hurt himself or was hiding. Either way, it made her sick to think of what might race through his head.

He was a sensitive boy and cared for her unconditionally. He'd been insisting he was the man of the house since he had no pa and got right angry if anyone spoke to her harshly. No matter how often she told Ben that he wasn't old enough to take on that responsibility, he had decided it was his duty.

Water boiled on the stove. Jacob would want a hot pot of coffee when he returned, and she'd like one as well. Besides, she always had warm coffee available for her boarders, although there weren't many inside her home that night. She had lost another customer that afternoon after Mrs. Greer's arrival. She didn't know if she could handle losing any more.

Jacob told her not to worry, but it was all she had done lately. She wasn't concerned with the lack of money. It was more the thought that she couldn't keep customers. Her cooking had improved over the past few years, but it still wasn't the best she'd ever tasted. The men didn't complain, but they didn't beg for second or third helpings either. She made delicious pastries, though, and those who stayed clamored for whatever she produced in that regard. Her cookies, cakes, and pies were quite delicious, if she said so herself.

She'd considered selling the pastries at the Saturday market, but she wasn't sure if she had the time. Ben kept her busy with his endless shenanigans, and most nights, her head barely hit the pillow before she was fast asleep. She wasn't sure she could find the time to bake what she'd need to make a profit.

The back door creaked open. Ben tried to sneak in, scampering to the door leading to the hallway. She shook her head. The little rascal looked like he'd been through the wringer, but relief at him being home subdued her anxiety. Jacob must've tried to clean him, but there was no hiding the rips in both his shirt and trousers. That boy went through countless clothes. It was a wonder she didn't go broke from having to replace them every time she turned around.

"Stop right there, young man," she said.

Ben jumped and looked up at her with a guilty expression on his face.

"Where have you been?"

"Outside," he mumbled.

Frannie shook her head. "Benjamin, don't be coy with me. Where have you been?"

His right foot circled the floor, and his shoulders were slumped, but he kept quiet.

Sighing, she pulled out a kitchen chair and sat facing him. "Come here."

He moved as slow as a snail across the room before he stood right in front of her.

She took his hands in hers. "Mrs. Greer came to visit me this afternoon."

Tears fell down his cheeks, and her heart broke. Ben did not deserve what that woman had done to him. She could only imagine the hurtful words she had yelled.

"It's all right. I'm not mad at you."

"I know you ain't mad at me, Momma, but you's gonna be mad at Mrs. Greer, and then she'll... she'll..." He couldn't continue as his little body shook with sobs.

She pulled him into her arms. "Oh, baby, it's all right. There's nothing she can do to either of us. She's an unhappy lady and just doesn't like children."

He swiped at his tears and raised his big brown eyes to her, the spitting image of his father. "I know she don't like me, Momma, but what if she hurts you?"

Frannie hated the pain her son dealt with on account of mean-spirited people in town. "Ben, sweetheart, she can't hurt me, not as long as I have you by my side."

He wrapped his arms around her neck and held tight. "I'm sorry I made her mad. We was just playing in the pond, and then that stupid Willie told me I was a ba... bas..." He shook his head. "I don't know how to say it, Momma, but he said I had no pa, and that you were a... a fallen woman and that she was gonna put you in outer darkness."

Frannie's heart splintered into a million pieces.

"I don't know what that means, but it didn't sound good. I don't want her saying mean things about you."

Frannie squeezed her son tight. She'd lied about her past to keep her son safe, and it hadn't done them any good. Somehow, someone had labeled Ben as a bastard, and there was no way to stop it. Rumors, once started, never stopped. She might have to leave Virginia City if people believed Ben was one. There was no way she could allow her son to be treated that way, not if she had anything to do about it.

Eleven

Frannie pulled the blankets up to Ben's neck. His eyes were sleepy, and his thumb was stuck in his mouth. He tried so hard not to suck it when he was outside playing, but at night, he gave in and put it in his mouth for the comfort it provided him. She'd have to get him to stop, but after the day he'd had, she wouldn't mention it. He needed a soothing mother's care, not censure over something trivial.

"Sleep well, sweetheart," she said. "Everything will be all right in the morning."

He nodded, and a few seconds later, his eyes closed, sleepiness overtaking him.

She sat and watched him. The rise and fall of his chest gave her immense reassurance. She wasn't sure what she was going to do about Mrs. Greer and her mistreatment of Ben, though. He didn't deserve the anger and had only been following the lead of the older boys he'd been playing with.

Frannie felt bad Ben had been part of those who had torn apart her flower garden. She'd take Ben over there in a few days to see if he could help right the damage. It was too late in the season to replant, but they could at least clean up the mess and tell her they would plant bulbs and seeds in the spring. Frannie didn't think Mrs. Greer would be satisfied, but it was the only thing she could think of to make things right.

Sighing, she rubbed at her eyes. It had been a long day, and it wasn't over yet. She still had plenty to do before she could sleep, so there would be no closing her eyes for quite some time. Being mindful not to wake Ben, she pulled the blankets higher on his chest and left his room. The lantern gave her enough light that she left his room without tripping over the toys he'd left scattered. She would encourage him to clean up his mess in the morning, but for now, she'd leave it be.

Leaving his door cracked so he wouldn't become frightened in the middle of the night, she tiptoed toward the back staircase. Jacob was likely in the kitchen warming his dinner. She had left him to his own devices, but he told her he preferred it that way. He didn't like to be fussed over, and if he had his way, he'd likely be sleeping and eating in the mountains somewhere. She had tried to encourage him to leave, but he insisted on staying and helping, claiming he would go when it was time. She just didn't know when he thought that time was.

There were plenty of nights when she would step outside and catch him on a chair next to the barn, staring toward the mountains, a piece of hay stuck in his mouth. He claimed he was just resting, but she saw the longing in his eyes to leave the hustle and bustle of the town behind him. He'd much rather be hunting and living in the mountains. That had been his dream, the one Cole had told her about years ago.

Cole had confided in her one night after the war had ended. They had been drinking to the end of the killing, and in trying to distract her, Cole told her stories about men at the mine. He had regaled her with story after story of what men had told him over the years, especially when the war was ravaging so much heartache on everyone and their families. No one had been immune to the fighting.

Jacob had fought in the war, but he'd come looking for a job like many of those who'd survived. He and Cole had become fast friends, and Jacob had told Cole about his dream of becoming a fur trapper. While that life was not as fruitful as it had been in years past, he had wanted to see the West and all that it offered. He was excited at the thought of exploring the Rocky Mountains and told Cole that once he saved enough, he was going to explore.

When Jacob left Pennsylvania, it had been the same day she had gathered her belongings to flee. Running into him had been a blessing for her but not for him. He'd felt obligated to stay on once he discovered she was pregnant. She carried an enormous amount of guilt in knowing she was the reason he couldn't live the life he wanted. But he wouldn't leave until he was ready, and there was no way she could change his mind.

Frannie had tried over the years to get him to chase after his dream, but he was stubborn and refused to go. The only thing that gave her a measure of comfort was that Jacob cared for Ben and would do anything to make her little boy happy. She would be forever grateful for him and everything he had done for her. One day, she would convince him to do as he really wanted.

She opened the kitchen door and found Jacob right where she expected him to be. His head was buried in the pantry, looking for more food. He had an appetite that rivaled a week's worth of boarders. She tried to make sure he had at least double what she served her boarders, but sometimes it wasn't enough. He was a large, muscular man and had grown more so in the years he had arrived with her in Virginia City.

"Did you find your dinner?" she asked, walking to the counter where the bags of flour and sugar sat waiting for her. She groaned internally. While she had plenty to do, she'd rather just sit and rest her feet, but there was no time for that and no reason to ruminate on what she wished she could do. She had given up that ability when she opened a boarding house. The men staying there were guaranteed a nice breakfast and dinner. She didn't serve the midday meal and was glad she'd never agreed to that. If she had, she would've spent all day in the kitchen, and nothing else would've gotten accomplished.

Jacob turned around, looking sheepish, his arms full of a cake she had made just that morning. She shook her head and laughed. The man was predictable. He had a tremendous sweet tooth, and she hadn't hidden the cake as well as she had thought. Usually, she kept them stuffed in various nooks and crannies, but she'd left him alone in the kitchen for far too long.

"Uh, yes, but I was also looking for something for my friend out there, and well, I couldn't help but notice this in the pantry." He held up the cake in front of him as though she wouldn't knock him upside the head, since he was holding the precious bundle in his arms.

"Friend?" she said, taking the cake from his hands and placing it on the table. It was a good thing she had made not one but two cakes that morning. Either he hadn't found the second one or he thought it'd be best to leave it be. She did have a temper at times.

"Yes, he's well..." He paused. "He's waiting outside."

"Would he like to come in?"

"Ah, no, no. I think it's best if we sit outside. I'm a bit dirty and don't want to mess up your clean chairs."

She eyed him closely and raised an eyebrow at his obvious lie, but she wouldn't question him. He had a right to his privacy. She wouldn't ask questions he didn't want to answer.

After pulling two clean plates from the shelf, she cut two large slices and then put both plates on a tray. "Would you and your friend care for some coffee?"

He nodded and rocked back and forth on his feet, looking everywhere but at her. She nudged him away from the wood stove and picked up the hot pot. It had sat warming and would serve them well. Quick as could be, she filled two coffee mugs and placed them next to the slices of cake.

"Sugar? Milk?"

"No, thank you, Frannie. That looks mighty tasty." He licked his lips.

"Who's your friend?"

He stumbled back, as if she had just interrogated him.

"What's wrong?" she asked.

"Ah, nothing, nothing at all." He swiped at his hair, pushing it back behind his ear.

He looked guilty. She guessed he'd found the cookies in the pantry and had a few of those too, but she wouldn't reprimand him for that. He'd brought Ben home safe, so if he wanted to keep the cookies a secret, who was she to say a word? It was a small price to pay for him being such a godsend to both her and Ben.

She picked up the tray and started toward the door when he ripped it from her hands, the coffee sloshing over the sides of the mugs. "What in the world, Jacob? I could've burned you with that hot coffee."

"Sorry, sorry. Didn't mean to startle you. I just... I can take it. No need for you to do that. I'm sure you have plenty to do." He crept backward before pushing open the door with his hip, and before she could say a word, he had slipped away.

She shook her head, a grin on her lips. Whatever he was up to, she wouldn't question. He was right about one thing--she had too much to do. If he wanted to serve his friend, then she'd let him. If she didn't get started on the fixings for the morning meal, she'd be up way past her bedtime, and then she'd surely be cranky in the morning, and that wouldn't do.

Lumbering to Cole's side, Jacob dropped a tray on the table between the two chairs. The light from the kitchen highlighted what looked like two pieces of chocolate cake and mugs of coffee. Cole could smell the roasted coffee beans, and it was a welcome scent. He hadn't had a decent cup in days. It'd be nice to sit back and enjoy it, although he needed to speak with the owner of the boarding house to see if she had any rooms available. Jacob had told him she did and that he'd take care of it, but he'd rather talk to her and make sure the boy was all right as well.

"That looks mighty tasty, Jacob," Cole said.

Jacob grinned and plopped into a chair. "Oh, it will be, trust me. Her cakes and pies are to die for. She hides them from me 'cause she knows I have a mighty big ole sweet tooth. She left me in the kitchen by myself for far too long, and I found the one she made this morning."

"Mrs. Black won't mind that I'm having a piece?"

"Who?" Jacob asked.

"Mrs. Black."

Jacob fumbled for the plates, his movements jerky. "Oh, yes, Mrs. Black. She won't mind at all. She's the one who sliced 'em up for us. I told her I had a friend outside. She was happy to give us a piece after I came out of the pantry with the cake in my hands, of course."

Cole shook his head. Jacob had changed little in the intervening years outside of gaining broader shoulders and becoming more muscular. "Virginia City's been good to you."

Jacob shoved a piece of cake into his mouth and chewed, pure contentment on his face. After a moment, he swallowed and smacked his lips. "Yes, it has been. Although truth be told, I'd much rather be up in those mountains." He pointed his chocolate-covered fork toward the peaks in the distance.

"I'm surprised you're still in town, truth be told," Cole said. "I thought for sure when you left Pennsylvania, you'd finally head to the mountains. You'd always said that was what you wanted to do."

Jacob placed the plate on his knee and pushed back on the chair, resting it on its back two legs. He lifted a foot and dropped it on the railing. "That'd been the plan, but then, circumstances being what they may, I stayed. Fra... I mean, Mrs. Black needed help, and once I saw that little one, I couldn't leave 'em alone."

"Ben told me he doesn't have a pa."

Jacob looked over the yard, his gaze thoughtful. "No, he doesn't. She doesn't like to talk about it and says he died of the influenza."

"That's a shame. The storekeeper told me as such when I stopped in at the mercantile to ask for a recommendation on where to stay. I forgot to ask him about you, but I guess fate was looking out for me. I couldn't believe it when I saw you walking out of the barn with Ben."

"He is something, ain't he?" Jacob said, his face brightened. "The little monkey is a joy, but he has so much energy he near drives her to distraction. He needs a pa, but she ain't willing to look for a husband. I think she's still in love with his pa."

"What about you and her?" Cole asked.

"What?" Jacob said, choking on the piece of cake he had just put into his mouth. "No, nope, not gonna happen."

Cole laughed at the horrified expression on Jacob's face. It was as if Cole had just surprised Jacob with the biggest secret he could've ever revealed.

"And why not?" Cole asked, seeing if he could get a bigger rise out of his friend.

Jacob dropped the plate on the table and stood. He shoved his hands into his back pockets and stood on the edge of the steps, staring into the distance. "She's a beautiful woman, don't get me wrong, but I don't need a wife and never planned on having one."

"Then why are you here?"

Jacob didn't answer, his shoulders tensing with the question.

"I don't mean to pry, but when you left Pennsylvania, I thought you were going west."

"I did." There was an undertone to Jacob's voice that Cole didn't understand.

"I didn't expect to find you working for a woman running a boarding house," Cole said.

"Didn't expect it either, truth be told, but she needed the help, and I couldn't leave her be. It didn't seem right." Jacob crossed his arms across his chest and turned back to look at Cole. "There's something I need to tell you."

Cole looked over the rim of his mug of coffee and caught Jacob's eye. Instead of taking a sip, he placed the mug of coffee down. "You sound serious."

"I... Shit." He ran his fingers through his hair, his expression tight. "I didn't expect it to happen this way."

"What to happen, what way?" Foreboding crawled across Cole's shoulder blades. He tensed, waiting for Jacob to tell him what was wrong.

"When I sent you that letter, I thought..." He pounded his fist on the railing of the porch. "I thought I was doing the right thing."

"Jacob, whatever it is, it can't be that horrid. There was nothing wrong with encouraging me to come out here. I had nothing in Pennsylvania, not after Frannie left."

Jacob's eyes grew alarmed.

What did I say?

"I'm glad you sent me the letter," Cole said. "I have a chance at a new life. Maybe now I can move on and forget about her. I have to let her go."

Jacob swallowed a few times before he spoke. "Well, about that--"

"Jacob, where are you?"

The door to the kitchen opened. It was the woman he had dreamed about for years, the one he could never forget. It was Frannie with a lantern in her hand and a charming smile on her face.

"Are you and your friend..." She turned her head and looked straight at him. Her smile dropped and shock rippled across her face.

Twelve

September 2, 1870

Cole rolled over on the four-poster bed where Jacob had deposited him the night before. He hadn't slept and instead had tossed and turned, wondering what the hell he'd gotten himself into. Cole had dreamed he would see Frannie again, but not like this.

When she stepped onto the porch, he'd scrambled to stand and then uttered but a few words to her. He had been taken aback to find her after so many years apart. She was the same, except for the evident panic in her eyes and furtive movements. She hadn't been prepared to see him, just as he hadn't been prepared to see her. So many questions crossed his mind, but he'd muttered something incoherent before she disappeared inside the house.

Jacob had been quiet, quickly showing him to a room, telling him they'd talk more in the morning before leaving him alone. Jacob likely sensed the rage building inside of Cole and didn't want to be near him when he blew.

Cole hoped he wasn't the type of man to let his anger override his sense of decency, but he wasn't sure he could control it, not this time. Jacob had known where Frannie had gone and had come with her as far as he could tell. They had both left at the same time, although Cole had never put it together, as he had never been quite sure of the day that Frannie left. Had they betrayed him? Had they left together? He didn't know what to think, and it had kept him up throughout the long night.

A door slammed, and squeals of laughter and running feet were outside his door. It sounded like Ben. Suddenly, the door to his room pushed open, and a small body careened onto his bed.

"Benjamin," Frannie yelled, but she was too late. Ben had found him.

Cole couldn't help but smile at the rambunctious little boy who had jumped into his bed. He sat and grabbed the boy before he could bounce right off it.

"Cole, you stayed the night!" Ben yelled.

"Benjamin, you come here right this instant. You woke Mr. Seymour and likely everyone else in this house." Frannie's voice was harsh, and Ben's face fell.

"It's all right, Frannie," Cole said. "No harm done."

She glared at him, and he felt the full censure of her gaze, just as much, if not more so, than Ben. Ben had climbed into Cole's lap and promptly stuck his thumb in his mouth, the sucking sounds the only noise in the room. Frannie stood at the foot of his bed, looking more beautiful than he remembered. Her face had thinned, her hips were wider, and even her breasts looked slightly plumper, but her arms looked strong. She was wearing a loose calico skirt and a thin cotton shirt that shouldn't have made his heart race uncontrollably like a bee humming toward a hive, but it did.

Cole had missed her, and his gut twisted with both anger and desire. He didn't know how to act around her or what to do. He hadn't expected to ever see her again, and now he was under her roof with her son in his arms.

Her son!

He looked at Ben, eyeing him differently than he had the day before. The thought of Ben being his had briefly crossed his mind while he tried to sleep, but Frannie wasn't that cruel and wouldn't have done that to him. She had known how he felt about fathering a child.

Frannie must've gotten with child by someone else, but who? He couldn't imagine who. Unless Ben was Jacob's? He wanted to ask, and he would get answers from Frannie, but not now and not in front of Ben. If Ben was his, there would be hell to pay, but he wouldn't yell at Ben's mother in front of him. The boy was protective of her, and the last thing he wanted was for Ben to think of him in the same way as Mrs. Greer. They had formed a friendship of sorts, and he wanted to keep it that way, especially if the boy in his arms was his son.

His son. The thought made his heart soar with joy while at the same time bubble over with anger if Frannie had hidden the truth from him.

Ben snuggled close to Cole as though being near him would save him from his mother's wrath.

"Benjamin," Frannie said. "Come here."

Ben shook his head, keeping his eyes closed tight as though knowing if he looked at his mother, he'd have to obey her.

"Ben," Cole said.

He turned his head and looked up at Cole.

"I think you better do as your mother says."

"I don't wanna," he mumbled around his thumb.

"Benjamin," Frannie warned. "You will get off Mr. Seymour's bed this instant and go to your room."

Ben's eyes filled with tears, but he seemed resigned to his task. He climbed off Cole's lap and slid to the floor. His footsteps dragged across the wooden boards until he got near his mother. Instead of going toward her, he scooted around her and ran out of the room and down the hall. A door slammed a moment later.

"He will surely be the death of me," she muttered, seemingly talking to herself.

"Will he?" Cole chuckled softly. Ben was a precocious little boy.

Frannie's gaze flew toward him, and she cringed. "No, I'm sorry. I shouldn't have said that. He's a good boy but sometimes forgets that we don't live alone in the house." She pushed back her hair and straightened her blouse, her eyes raking over his bare chest. She blushed. "I'm sorry, I shouldn't be in here." She started to back out of the room.

"No, Frannie. Don't leave. We need to talk."

She shook her head, stumbling, but he scrambled out of bed and grabbed her before she could leave. He was wearing a set of drawers so he wasn't completely in the nude, but from the way she was blushing, she likely thought he had been. She pulled from his arms which gave him enough time to slam the door shut.

He leaned against it and crossed his arms over his chest. She eyed him and retreated to the other side of the room. She was stuck inside with him, and the sweat across her brow told him she wasn't prepared for this conversation, but he was.

"I think it's time we talked, don't you, Francesca?"

Frannie stood on the other side of the room, eyeing Cole. He never called her Francesca. He was furious, and his anger was directed at her. She couldn't blame him. Frannie had seen it in his eyes when he had put two and two together. She could deny it, but it was too easy to do the math. Jacob wouldn't lie for her, and Ben would be quick to tell anyone how old he was and when he was born. He knew the story and often told others about the day he was born, being right proud of himself for putting his mother through hell. A moment of pain that had brought her immense joy from the day he was placed in her arms until now, even when he was yelling and screaming, carrying on so much so that boarders would leave after they couldn't take his noisy and rambunctious playing.

Her hands shook and sweat dripped down her neck and under her arms as Cole continued to stare at her, not saying a word. He wouldn't hurt her, at least not physically, but she wasn't sure she could handle his outrage or disdain. He would hate her for what she'd done, but she'd thought she had no choice. She hadn't realized she was pregnant until long after she had left Pennsylvania. She believed she was saving him from a future he didn't want, but he wouldn't appreciate her reasoning, at least not until his temper had cooled and even then she wasn't sure he ever would.

Frannie straightened her shoulders when the silence became too much to bear. "Say what you need to. I can't leave Ben unsupervised for too long. He'll frighten away what boarders I do have left with his playing. I also need to put breakfast on the table." She raised a hand to her forehead, trying without success to hide her tremors.

Cole looked like he had cracked a smile, but he hid it before she could tell for sure. He pushed away from the door, and her gaze zoomed in on his bare chest. He wore a pair of drawers that hung low on his hips, and her skin tingled with memories she had shoved down to her most secret place. It was only when she was alone, and everything was quiet, that she allowed herself to remember that night.

He walked toward her like a cat stalking a mouse, but instead of coming close, he abruptly turned and sat on the small settee, his gaze unrelenting. She almost wished he had hit her. It would hurt less than the nonchalant manner he appeared to have, although she supposed he'd had all night to think about what to say to her, even if he had just realized that Ben was his.

"Are you going to sit, Frannie, or continue to stand there like you're afraid I'm gonna hit you?"

"I know you wouldn't hit me, Cole Seymour," she snapped. There was no way she would admit she had just thought he would.

"Then sit." He waved to the chair across from him.

She didn't want to be anywhere near him because she might lose her nerve and jump into his arms if he gave her half a chance. He was furious, and while he tried to hide it, she was sure he had many questions. Questions she had avoided for over five years, and now she was going to have to face the truth.

"I'm fine standing where I'm at." She wasn't. Her legs shook under her skirt, but she would be strong and show no panic, for his discovery of her most precious secret was enough of a humiliation.

"We've known each other too long for us to be like this. Please... sit."

She grabbed a blue afghan off the bed, threw it into his lap, and plopped into the chair across from him. "At least cover yourself. It's improper that I'm in a gentleman's room and would be made worse if anyone were to see you half undressed."

He picked up the afghan and threw it over his shoulders, his mocking grin unmistakable.

Her neck bristled. "This isn't funny."

"I never said it was," he drawled. "You're looking well."

He wouldn't distract her. "Thank you. Why are you here?"

He shook his head. "Getting straight to the point, I see." His mocking grin fell into a thin line, his expression shuddering.

"There's no point in us pussyfooting around this, don't you think?"

He chuckled. "Pussyfooting, huh?"

Heat crawled up her chest. She hadn't meant it the way it sounded. "You're a scoundrel."

"So be it, but at least I didn't leave Pennsylvania in the dead of night without telling a soul where I was going," he snapped.

She shrunk in her chair. The censure in his eyes was painful to see. He wasn't wrong, but he didn't understand and never would. "I had no choice." Her voice was low.

"You had plenty of choices. You left without telling me where you were going. We were friends." His gaze was pointed and direct. He wasn't going to let her out of this conversation, no matter how much she desired it.

"I had my reasons." Reasons he would never understand.

"One of which is that young boy you gave birth to."

Acid rose in her throat, making her want to gag. If she had eaten this morning, she was sure she would have lost it all over the floor. Instead, she swallowed multiple times, trying to contain what was there. She raised a hand to her lips, a nervous twitch to them. "I don't know what you're talking about."

"Don't play us both for a fool, Francesca Collins." His voice lashed out. "That little boy is my son, isn't he?"

Frannie's mouth fell open in horror. Her worst nightmare was playing out in front of her. She could deny it, but there had already been too many lies between them. He deserved to know the truth.

She nodded slightly, and a disappointed scowl crossed his lips. His hands pulled at the afghan in his lap, a visible reminder of what he had looked like when she had asked him all those years ago to give her a child. That time, he had practically shredded a sofa pillow.

He took a visible deep breath before relaxing his grip on the afghan. "Why didn't you tell me?"

"By the time I discovered I was with child, I was already here in Virginia City, and I didn't..." She paused. "I didn't see the point in ruining your life."

He slammed a fist on the arm of the chair. "You didn't see the point! You kept me from my son!"

She cringed at the force of his fury. "I'm sor--"

He abruptly stood. The chair fell behind him and slammed to the ground. He kicked it out of his way. "No, don't tell me you're sorry!" His voice roared in the small room.

Frannie wanted to run, hide, but she couldn't. She was trapped. He stood feet from her, his face boiling red with rage, his body stiff as though he was holding back from springing on her and tearing her limb from limb.

A loud knock sounded on his bedroom door. Cole muttered cuss words at the interruption but didn't move to open it.

The door pushed open, and Jacob stepped inside, glaring at them both. "You need to lower your voice, Cole. You're scaring Ben. He's worried sick that you're hurting his ma."

"I would never--"

"Right now, that doesn't matter. He's crying and shaking with panic. He wanted to come in here to protect his ma. So, whatever this is"--Jacob waved his hands--"needs to stop."

"She kept him from me, Jacob." Cole's voice broke.

Frannie's guilt grew with every word out of Cole's mouth. She had kept Ben hidden, but she'd thought she was doing the right thing.

"That don't matter now," Jacob said. "All that matters is that little boy."

"Did you know?" Cole asked.

Jacob crossed his arms against his chest, his legs spread, his face expressionless. "Does it really matter if I did?"

"Of course it matters," Cole roared.

"I said, keep your voice down. I won't have any problem silencing you if it'll keep him from hurting any further," Jacob said, his voice low but his intent clear.

Cole seemed to shrivel at those words. He stalked to the wardrobe, yanked open the door, and pulled out a shirt. His movements were abrupt.

"What are you going to do, Cole?" Frannie asked. She was afraid of the answer, but she had to know.

He turned and glared at her. "I'm going to go talk to *my* son and reassure him."

"No," she said, scrambling to stand. "You're not going anywhere near him, not when you're angry with me." She scooted around the chairs and ran out the door.

"Frannie, get back here," Cole yelled, but she ignored him.

Her son was her priority, not the man who stood furious over the choices she had made. She would protect Ben, no matter the cost to herself.

Thirteen

September 3, 1870

Frannie leaned over the gelding's neck as it raced along the open field. It galloped as though the forces of hell were at its feet, licking, biting, devouring until it could run no more. She didn't want to stop, but his sides heaved with exertion. She had pushed the horse too far. She exhaled, leaned back, and pulled the reins just enough for the horse to slow to a sedate gait. While she didn't want to return to her responsibilities back at the boarding house, she couldn't ignore them for much longer.

She rested in the saddle and pushed away the strands of hair that had fallen across her cheeks. The horse ambled to a stop near a stream. He was likely as thirsty as she was hot. She dismounted, her back, shoulders, and neck sweaty from both the heat and the exertion of trying to run from her past. She had needed the reprieve from the censure she had received the day before. Ben would get the father he had always wanted, but she stood to lose Ben to the same man.

Wrapping the reins around a low-hanging branch, she knelt and pushed her skirts out of the way. Dropping her hands into the cool water, she let them rest for a long moment before cupping them together and bringing the water to her lips. Taking long drinks, she did it a few more times until her thirst was satisfied. She grabbed a handkerchief stuffed in the bosom of her blouse and drenched it before wiping away the sweat on her cheeks, chest, and back of her neck. It helped reduce the redness developing from the hot, scorching sun.

Her gaze focused on the water running across the boulders and riverbed in front of her. It had been a hot summer, and the water levels had dropped, but there was still enough rushing in front of her to soothe her battered soul. She wasn't sure it was enough, though, to calm the turmoil in her life. After she served breakfast to her boarders that morning, she had escaped out the backdoor following another disagreement with Cole.

There was no denying Ben was Cole's, and now Cole could take him from her. A part of her knew Cole was not cruel and wouldn't rip a child from his mother's arms, but he had every right to exact retribution on her. She had kept his son away from him for four long years. She had believed she was doing the right thing, or at least that was what she told herself so she could sleep well at night.

A horse neighed behind her, and tingles along her spine told her Cole had found her once again. He was a moth after a flame, not leaving her be and trying without success to defeat her. Bracing her hands on her knees, she stood and turned to face him. She'd jump in his arms without a second thought if she knew he wanted her, but alas, he did not. He hadn't five years ago, and he didn't now.

Cole stood behind her, a concerned yet kind look on his face. She bristled, knowing he was acting as though nothing had changed when everything had.

"Are you all right, Frannie? You ran out of the house so fast, I thought your feet were on fire." A knowing smirk crossed his lips.

"I'm fine," she said, brushing at her skirt. Nothing lined the dark brown fabric, but it kept her hands and eyes busy.

"You could've been hurt riding away like you did."

"Don't you worry about me, Cole Seymour. I've been taking care of myself for years. I know what I can handle and what I cannot." Her tone growled.

He held up his hands as though to ward off her ire. His efforts to placate her only irritated her further. "I realize that, but when you flew out of the house and pushed that poor horse like the devil himself was after you, it could've endangered him as well as yourself."

He was right, but she'd be damned if she'd admit it. "As you can see, we're both perfectly intact. No harm done." She waved to the horse, and he proved her point. The horse's muzzle nestled in the water, his chest no longer heaving from the pounding she'd put him through.

"Maybe not now but––"

"Enough," Frannie snapped. "I don't want to do this. You are not my father, nor my husband."

His face turned bright red. "And who decided that, may I ask?"

Her shoulders tensed, and all the frustration, angst, and fear came roaring out. "Yes, it was me. Are you happy?" she yelled. "I left without telling you and never told you that you had a son. What was I supposed to do?"

"Fran––"

"No, don't you Frannie me, Cole." She slammed a tight fist into the tree trunk next to her. Pain shot up her arm, but it was a fair punishment for her actions. "I was cornered, frightened, and didn't know what to do." Her fist relaxed, and she rested both hands against the rough bark, letting it scratch her gloveless hands. "I made the best decision I could. Was it the right one? I don't know. I'll never know because here we are today." Her chest rose and fell with suppressed rage at herself for making the decisions she'd made when other factors had forced her from her home in Pennsylvania.

Cole placed his hand on her shoulder, but she shrugged it away.

"Don't touch me." She was barely holding on to her composure. She feared she'd burst into tears if he so much as gave her an opening.

He was relentless and didn't listen to her, yet she shouldn't be surprised. He always knew what she needed, even if she didn't know it herself. It was one of many reasons why she loved him with everything in her. Over the years, she'd tried to convince herself that what she felt on that fateful night had been nothing but a desperation to have a child and not a chance to have one precious moment with him.

He pulled her back against his chest and wrapped his powerful arms around her waist, being gentle and doing his best not to crowd her. Resting his chin lightly against the top of her head, he just held her while the hot tears she'd tried to keep at bay ran unheeded down her cheeks.

"I've missed you, Frannie, more than you'll ever know."

She sniffled but kept quiet. There were no words she could say to make this debacle better.

"We really need to talk..."

She tried to pull away. She didn't want to do this again, but he didn't let go and instead just held fast.

"We've only argued since I arrived, and it's causing you to--"

She pushed at his arms and whirled around, placing her hands on his chest to keep him at arm's length. "Causing me to do what?"

His lips turned into a frown, his eyebrows scrunching together. "I misspoke."

"No, you didn't. You've never misspoken a day in your life. You've always known your mind and what you've wanted to say. Your overabundant confidence has always been an irritation, and yet I've always been jealous of that. I've always wanted to have as much courage as you, so don't tell me you misspoke. Don't lie to me now." She cringed as soon as she said it. She shouldn't have said that. "I'm sorry. I have no right to tell you not to lie when I've done it for years."

She tried to brush past him, but he didn't let her. Instead, he grabbed her elbow and forced her to stop.

"I won't lie to you then," he said.

She ripped her elbow from his grasp, wrapped her arms around her waist, and glared at him. "Then don't."

He shook his head. "Have you always been this contrary, or did I just forget about it?"

Frannie didn't answer him. She wasn't going to, no matter how long he stared at her.

Cole took off his hat and ran his fingers through the brown strands, sending a rush of longing through her. She had never forgotten how the silky waves felt against her fingertips, nor the taste of his lips against hers. Frannie loved him, but once again her heart was going to break as he didn't love her and never had.

"Why are you here?" she asked.

"I've asked myself that question multiple times. I didn't know you were here. Honestly, I'm not sure I would've come if I'd known." He paced in front of her, then halted. "That's a lie. If I'd known where you were, I would've dropped everything to find you. When you left, I was angry, frustrated, sad, and then lonely. As the days passed and no one knew where you'd gone, I felt like I'd lost my mind and my heart." Bracing his hands against his hips, he stood firm, his legs spread, his gaze unreadable. "I was clueless about what I had until you were gone."

She'd been observing him, but she avoided his direct gaze until he said those words. "What do you mean?" She hadn't wanted to believe a small part of him had missed her and perhaps felt more than friendship.

He reached for her hands, but she stumbled back. There was

no way she would let him touch her. If she did, there was no telling what she might do. Her emotions were cascading down a dangerous slope, gathering speed toward the bottom until the world would either fall out from beneath her or catch her and lift her up to a bliss so wonderful, she'd only have the dreams of what might be to sustain her.

"Have we grown so far apart that you won't let me touch you?" His eyes were filled with the same need that she was sure shined in her own.

"It's not that," she mumbled. "If you touch me, I'm afraid of what I'll do."

His head tilted to the side, and a slow smile crossed his lips. "So, you're afraid of what you'll do? I believe I might need to see what that is." He took a few steps forward, but she retreated.

On one hand, she didn't appreciate the look in his eyes. On the other, it excited her. Giggling, she grabbed her skirts and whirled around, taking off at a run. She hadn't played in years, but the moment turned playful, and she would enjoy it for as long as it lasted. He growled behind her, but it was a hungry growl, not an angry one. Laughing until her sides ached, she ran between the trees, darting from one to another while he pretended he couldn't catch her. It reminded her of many games they had played as children, although it'd usually involved her chasing him, not the other way around.

Frannie raced, dodging bushes, seedlings, and wide tree trunks until she stopped to catch her breath. She rested behind a large pine tree and leaned against it, the trunk wider than she was tall. Her breath came in quick gasps, and her heart pounded something fierce.

"Where, oh where, has my Frannie gone?" Cole chanted. His voice was far away and then came closer and closer.

She didn't dare turn. If she did, she might make enough of a sound he would catch her, although she was sure it would be welcome if he did.

"Boo," he said right next to her ear.

She screeched and again took off running, but it was too late. He snatched her by the waist and spun around with her in his arms. Laughing at their antics, he stopped when the world became too dizzy. He slowly but surely let her slide down his hard length. Her belly burned with a hunger she hadn't felt in years. A hunger she had only relived when she was alone in her room at night, when the sky was dark and the house was quiet.

He stepped around her until he faced her, his hands gentle as his fingers grazed against her arm, her shoulders, until they rested on the sides of her cheeks. He looked into her eyes, the pupils piercing but gentle at the same time.

"I love you, Frannie Collins."

Her heart stopped. Her mouth went dry. Her skin tightened.

His thumb brushed against her bottom lip. He hesitated, and when she didn't pull away, he bent his head and pulled her mouth into a soul-searing kiss that sent fire through her limbs, exploding out of her like a volcano blowing off its top.

He loved her.

Wait! No! No! She pulled away. He didn't love her. He couldn't love her. Cole only said those words because he wanted her son.

"No," she cried. "We can't do this. Not again. Not when I know you don't mean it the way I wish you did." A sob caught in her throat. She raised her fists to her mouth, her body shaking. Things were happening too fast and were out of her control.

A pained expression crossed his face. He raised his hands to stop her, but she pushed them away as she ran toward her horse. She had to leave. Standing near Cole, letting him touch her, was too much to bear. Her heart and soul couldn't take being torn apart again. It had taken her months to come to terms with losing him all those years ago. She couldn't go through that again.

Before she could mount her horse, he placed his hand over hers and another on her waist. His touch was tender as he uncurled her fingers from it. "Frannie, we should sit and talk. There have been too many misunderstandings between the two of us, especially if you don't believe what I say to you."

Her shoulders sagged. She wanted to trust and believe in him, but she didn't know if she had it in her. Too much hurt rested beneath the surface. She raised her gaze to his, saw the caring look in his eyes, and tried to remind herself that she had one reason to listen. Ben. It wasn't her son's cross to bear for the poor choices she had made. He deserved a father, and she had to give it to him. This man was waiting to step into the role that had belonged to him since the day Ben took his first breath.

"Please?" he asked again, his voice low.

She bowed her head and let him lead her to a fallen log. He took her hands and helped her to sit. In a different time, she would've pushed away his help. She wasn't helpless, but today she felt like a small child who had lost all sense of herself, and she supposed she had.

A white handkerchief dangled in front of her eyes, and while she hated that he knew her too well, she wasn't too stubborn to deny she needed it. She looked a fright and hated that he saw her this way.

"Thank you," she murmured.

Cole sank to the ground in front of her. He moved at a snail's pace, being careful not to frighten her any further than she clearly was. She was a mess, and they both knew it.

Cole rested his forearms against his bent knees. His hat rested high on his brow. The sun shined on him, accentuating the laugh lines at the corners of his eyes and his dark brown pupils. Eyes she had never forgotten.

He cleared his throat and opened his mouth, but she placed a finger across his lips, silencing him. His eyes twinkled, and before she could remove her hand, the tip of his tongue brushed against the pad of her finger. Gasping, she pulled her hand into her lap.

She was sure she had imagined that. He would never do such a thing.

They sat in silence, her heart hammering. She couldn't just sit there. She had stopped him from speaking, so she had to say something to fill the stillness.

"I'm sorry, Cole."

He placed his hand atop hers, his skin warm and soothing. "There's no reason for apologies, not anymore."

She shook her head and tried to pull away. "There are. I've made so many mistakes, but I thought I had no choice. I realize I should've reached out once I knew for sure I was with child, but I had convinced myself you'd be better off knowing otherwise. I knew you didn't love me, didn't want a wife, and didn't want a child. I'd placed an unfair burden on your shoulders."

She took a breath, shuddering from saying the words that had burned inside her for so long. She met his gaze. Frannie wanted to understand what he was thinking, but he showed nothing. Instead, he'd let her say what she needed without censure or interruption.

"Why did you leave Pennsylvania without first telling me what Henry and Mr. Archer were doing?"

She was startled by his words. "How did you know about that?"

He lifted a hand to his forehead and rubbed at the spot between his eyes. "I've had plenty of time to think over the past two days when we weren't arguing or sending each other dirty looks."

She laughed at that. He was right. The tension between them had been palpable. "We've made a mess of things, haven't we? Poor Ben doesn't know what is going on and has been acting up, likely to distract me from my wrath."

Cole's eyes darkened at the mention of their son, but he kept any angry retorts to himself. She shouldn't have mentioned Ben, but he was a significant part of her life, and there was no way to ignore that.

"After you left, I was angry. I couldn't see straight. I wanted to believe Carrie was wrong and that you would return. As the days and months passed, I realized that whatever happened to us couldn't have been the only reason you left, especially when Henry Davenport laid claim to the mine and your lawyer, Mr. Archer, didn't stop him." He shifted on the ground and extended a leg on the far side of the log, locking her into place. "I tried asking both of them what had happened to you, but neither knew, or at least that's what they claimed. They said it wasn't my business and to stay out of it or I'd find myself without a job and thrown into jail."

Frannie grimaced. "I wasn't thinking with clarity when I left. I was terrified that Henry was going to have me committed to the Lilies for the Mentally Insane."

"That's ridiculous. No one would've committed you." Cole's eyes darkened.

The thought of being committed had shaken her to her core. "You don't know that."

"I do," he lashed out.

"Cole, I know you would've tried to support me and fought to keep me from that institution, but Henry had Judge Smith on his side. You know they held more power than either of us."

"Fran––"

"No, don't. You don't understand. Someone saw you leaving my house that night and Henry found out. He would've ruined me, regardless. It was already a stain on my reputation when I stepped into my father's footsteps at the mine. No one thought it was proper for a lady to be running things." Her skin crawled. While the war changed so much of their lives, it hadn't moved in any way to help the women who were left without a father or a brother. She had been luckier than most, but in the end, it hadn't mattered. "I was able to get away with running the mine through the end of the war. Most men were too busy fighting, and the women were barely holding on to what they owned, but once it was over, the nasty rumors grew. Plenty of my father's old friends avoided me on the street, casting their gazes elsewhere. I was just too stubborn to realize what was happening until it was too late for me to liquidate and leave on my own terms."

"I don't understand how he got your father's mine, though. He has since run it into the ground and was on the verge of closing when I left."

Frannie's heart broke at her father's hard work going to waste, but she'd had to let the mine go when she left and couldn't claim it now. She sighed. She'd rather not reveal the horrifying truth about what her father had done, but there was no reason to keep the secrets any longer. "His will specified I was to have a child by my thirty-first birthday or the mine would go to Henry's father. As you know, Henry's father passed away months after my father. According to Mr. Archer, the mine would be Henry's if I didn't produce a child. Both Henry and Mr. Archer didn't think I had much hope of gaining a husband, let alone a child."

Cole's mouth hung open in shock, and it took him a moment to form the words. "We could've fought it in the courts."

Frannie twisted the handkerchief between her fingers. "I thought of that, but remember, with Henry's relationship with Judge Smith, I didn't stand a chance. There was no doubt that what Henry wanted, Henry would get. My only choice was to have a child, which is why I came to you."

"Why didn't you tell me"–– he pounded his fist into the hard ground––"that was the reason you wanted a child?"

"I was mortified. I had to ask my very best friend to... Well, you know." Her face was hot with embarrassment. After everything they'd shared, the resulting birth of their son should have eliminated the humiliation over this conversation, but she was still more innocent than she'd care to admit.

One night with Cole had left her wanting for more, but she'd never get it. No one would ever come close to comparing to Cole and if she couldn't have him, then she'd be alone for the rest of her life.

"I could have..." He held his head in his hands.

"After our night together, my guilt at making you sleep with me, especially when I knew you didn't want a child or a wife, made me realize that my only recourse was to sell the mine *if* I wanted to keep Henry from getting it." This was harder than she thought but she had to tell him. "A few days after you and I had..." She gulped. "A few days later, I went to Mr. Archer's home to ask him if he'd found anyone I could sell the mine to." Laurie had told Frannie it would take more than one time to get with child, but Frannie had been too caught up in wanting a child to realize the implications.

"We could have tried again, Frannie."

She held back a chuckle of despair. "Cole, be honest with yourself. You didn't want what I had asked."

"I offered to marry you."

"Yes, you did, but it was an offer made of obligation, not of love. You didn't want to marry. You certainly didn't love me." Her voice broke at the pain of knowing how he felt about her and how it wasn't what she wanted.

He scowled. "I just told you that I love you. Why won't you believe me?"

"I know you do, but you love me like a sister, your best friend." The words were hard to spit past her lips, but she had to say them so he would understand.

He shook his head, a pained expression crossing his face. "That's not true. You don't know how I feel."

"But I do. You told me on countless occasions when we were still friends and confidants that you wouldn't marry and take the chance that a woman would leave you like your ma had left your pa."

"I..." A stark and noticeable pain crossed his eyes before he looked away.

Frannie wasn't a fool. The pain he'd experienced when his ma had left both him and his pa was something she would never forget. She hated to remind him, but he had to understand why she'd left the way she had.

"I was waiting to speak with Mr. Archer when he was pulled away. Then Henry arrived and cornered me in Mr. Archer's parlor. That was when he told me that someone had seen you leave my house. If I didn't marry him, I was to be committed to the mental institution. The orderlies were to pick me up the next day if I didn't agree. I wasn't going to marry that man, so I ran."

Cole muttered curse words under his breath, things that a lady should not have heard, but words she'd heard far more than he likely realized. His ease in uttering them was reminiscent of years gone by when he'd always been comfortable expressing himself in her presence. No secrets or harsh words between them.

"I went straight to the bank, where the banker, Mr. Edwards, gave me what he could from my accounts. Mr. Archer had visited him that morning and warned him not to give me any of my money, but Mr. Edwards didn't listen and gave me what he could. I tried reaching out after Ben was born to get the rest, but by that time, Mr. Archer and Henry had already taken everything that was Father's. His hands were tied, and he couldn't. I lost everything of my father's because of those two men. That was when I took a bit of what I had left and opened the boarding house. Jacob was kind enough to stay on and help."

"Why was Jacob with you?"

"Pure luck, I suppose." She smiled at the memory of her surprise when she stepped off the train and found him standing there, his arms crossed, a stern expression on his face, but his eyes twinkling with mirth. He had always been a good friend to Cole but had turned into the best of friends to her. "We were on the same train. I saw him at first and tried to avoid him. I thought I'd succeeded until I reached the end of the line and had to board the stagecoach. He appointed himself my protector and has been with me ever since."

"I'm glad he helped you"––he pounded his fist against his chest––"but it should've been me instead."

Fourteen

C ole listened as Frannie told him all that had occurred before she left Pennsylvania. The knowledge that he hadn't been there for her was a burden he'd have to carry for the rest of his life. But he was frustrated that she wasn't listening to him now. What he said was true. He was thoroughly and completely in love with her.

He couldn't turn back time, but he hoped to change the future if she would only let him.

"Cole, so much has changed in these past few years. I'm a different woman than I was when we saw each other last."

"I know that. The changes are evident, and they've only made you more beautiful in my eyes."

She blushed, her hand fluttering to her chest. "I don't know about that."

"I do." He scrambled off his backside and onto his knees so he could look straight into her eyes. "I love you, Francesca Collins. I always have. I just didn't know what it was or what it meant until I saw you again."

"You're just feeling responsible for––"

"No. Don't tell me how I feel. I know my mind. While it

might've taken you leaving and me finding you again to realize what those feelings were, I did figure it out. I won't let you or anyone else tell me they are less than what they are."

She gulped and reached for his hand, curling her fingers around his.

"I love you," he said. "I love you more than words can say. I'll continue to tell you that every minute... of every day... for the rest of our lives."

Her eyes were wet with tears, hope blooming inside of her like a ripe berry. "I--"

"Cole! Frannie!"

A horse and rider rushed into the clearing, the horse neighing when the rider jerked him to a stop. It was Jacob, and the stark fear on his face sent apprehension through Cole's limbs. "There you are."

Cole jumped to his feet and helped Frannie stand.

"What is it?" Frannie asked. "Is something wrong in town?"

Jacob didn't waste any words. "It's Ben."

"What about Ben?" Frannie pulled away from Cole and tugged on Jacob's leg, her fingers clenching around his calf. "Is he hurt? Where is he? Why are you here?" Panic filled her eyes.

Placing his hands on her shoulders, Cole nudged her away from Jacob and his horse. "Frannie, let Jacob speak. I'm sure it's not as awful as you think." However, when Cole looked at Jacob, his expression told him it was worse than he could imagine.

"He's fallen into an old mine shaft."

"No!" Frannie scratched at Cole's hands. "Why are you here? Why aren't you trying to get him out?" She tried to pull away from Cole, but he held fast, this time holding her around the waist. He wouldn't let her hurt herself.

Jacob frowned, his eyes sad. "Men from town are trying to get to him. I'm too big to go down the shaft, and no one knew where you'd gone. The sheriff's working with men from the mines, trying to find someone small enough to go into the shaft."

"But you should've--"

"No, Frannie, stop. Jacob did right by coming to find us. We can stand here and ask questions, or we can get on our horses and head back." Cole sounded more reasonable than he felt inside. He couldn't lose Ben, not when he'd just found him.

She shuddered, then took a deep breath. "Yes, yes. You're right. I'm sorry, Jacob. I didn't mean to--"

"No, Fran. No need to apologize. Let's just get you back to town."

Cole led her to her horse and helped her to mount. Her hand rested on his, her eyes saying more in that moment than he could've ever hoped for. There would be a time and a place for the two of them to continue their conversation, but now wasn't it.

He mounted his horse, and a moment later, the three of them galloped back to town. Their ride was not as fast as Frannie's had been earlier that day but as fast as they could push their weary horses.

Thirty minutes later, they arrived at the mine shaft where his son had fallen. Men were shouting directions, running back and forth, pulling ropes, bringing in shovels and stacks of lumber. A wagon with a metal pulley had been found and was resting a few feet away from the shaft. A couple of men knelt behind the wagon wheels, placing large blocks of wood against them to keep it steady, while others were setting up a command station. It wasn't something they could tackle without careful thought. If they weren't careful, the mine shaft could collapse at any moment, and no one wanted to be responsible for that. A few women had gathered far from the action, looks of concern and fright on their faces as young boys stood huddled with them. Everyone's face was etched with fear and anxiety.

The sheriff knelt next to what Cole presumed was the mine shaft opening. He raised his head when they arrived, and the look on his face was enough to chill Cole's blood. He had to be strong for Frannie and keep his fears at bay. There was only going to be one outcome, no matter what the men might think. He hadn't come this far to find his son, only to lose him in a horrifying accident.

Cole dismounted and reached for Frannie's waist. She barely glanced at him, her gaze focused on the hole in the ground that contained their son. He grabbed her hand, and the two of them hurried forward but paused when the sheriff crawled back a few feet, stood, and waved for them to stop.

"No, don't come any closer. The ground's not steady, and any significant weight will send more dirt into the hole."

"Is he alive?" Frannie asked.

The sheriff lifted a weary hand to his forehead. "We think so, but we haven't heard a sound from him in over ten minutes. He was crying and screaming for help, but—" He rubbed his eyes. "Then it stopped."

Frannie uttered a cry of despair and started to collapse. Cole stopped her descent by snatching her around the waist and holding her upright.

"Frannie, we aren't going to believe the worst, not until we know otherwise. He might've fallen asleep, or he's too scared to cry out any further. We don't know." He paused, his heart beating erratically. "And until we do, we're going to work on getting him out. He can't have you falling apart, not when he'll need you the most when he's free." Cole turned to Jacob and waved him forward. "I need you to go with Jacob to where it's safe. We don't need the ground collapsing any farther, nor have anyone else get hurt. I'm going to confer with the sheriff and the other men to see what our options are. Can you do that for me?"

She raised tear-filled eyes to his, held back a sob, and nodded. She gripped his shirt. "Please save him. He needs his father."

His throat closed with emotion. That was the first time she had acknowledged in front of witnesses that Ben was his. There had been no denying it once he looked at Ben with clear eyes, but he hadn't realized how much he needed Frannie to admit it.

Looking over her shoulder at what the men were doing, Frannie let Jacob lead her away from the hole in the ground where her son rested. The sheriff and Cole talked. Their heads were bent together, Cole's lips grim, his hands on his waist.

She wanted to be near the mine shaft, to let Ben know they would save him and not to lose hope. A part of her couldn't help but wonder if it was too late. She didn't want to think the worst, but if he had stopped crying, what did that mean?

Taking stock of the situation, she took a deep breath and decided she wouldn't be in the way, nor the cause of any added harm. She would do as Cole said. Jacob found a bench and encouraged her to sit. Her hands trembled, and she tried to hide them in her skirts.

"Would you care for something to eat?" Jacob asked.

"I don't think I can." Tears threatened to fall, but she blinked them back. Now wasn't the time. "What am I going to do?"

Jacob knelt, blocking her view of what the men were doing to save her son. His wide shoulders were like a strong, stalwart boulder. He was clearly trying to distract her, but nothing could protect her from the cruelty of what had happened.

Jacob rested his thick fingers on her knees, his touch light as a feather. He might be a large man, but he was also a warm and cuddly bear. He had the heart of a lion but the touch of a lamb, and outside of Cole, he was the closest person to her. When he decided to leave for sights unknown, she'd be devastated.

"You're going to take a deep breath and let me get you food and water. You need to keep your strength up for..." He swallowed, dropping his eyes to look at his hands before he raised them once again. "For whatever may come our way."

She nodded warily. "All right, but before you do that, tell me what happened, please."

He sighed. "There's no point in――"

"I need to know. Please hide nothing from me. We've been through too much over the past few years for you to hide the ugly truth, don't you agree?"

"All right. If you're sure?"

"I am." Deep inside, her belly churned with all the horrible possibilities.

"I don't have all the details, but it sounds as though he and a bunch of the local boys were playing around the mine shaft. It'd been covered with a few pieces of wood and likely had been secured, but whatever held them in place had loosened over time. One boy thought it'd be fun to look inside, so they pulled the wood away to reveal the opening. They were throwing rocks and such into the hole when Mrs. Greer came upon them."

Frannie scowled. If Mrs. Greer was involved, then it'd been ugly. "She has never warmed up to Ben, I'm afraid."

He smiled, although it wasn't one of warmth. "I don't think she intended for any harm to come to him, but her wrath is legendary. The older boys knew well enough to stay away from her grip. Unfortunately, she got hold of Ben once again and was going to drag him back to the house when he pulled away and ran straight toward the open hole. It sounds as though he was afraid of what you might do. One of the older boys heard him yell to her that his momma was not a..." He avoided looking her in the eye.

"That I wasn't what?" Although she could imagine the harsh words Mrs. Greer would utter in Ben's presence.

"No reason to get into that. Suffice it to say, he wasn't looking and ran straight for the hole and fell inside. None of the older boys were close enough to stop or grab him as he fell. They ran for help while one stayed behind, yelling to Ben, telling him help was coming. Unfortunately, the ground grew unsteady."

"Where did Mrs. Greer go?" She had looked at those helping and congregating when they had arrived, and she didn't see the woman lurking nearby.

"The boy who stayed with Ben said she scurried off as soon as

Ben fell, likely to hide her shame in the part she played." Jacob's voice was filled with malice. It was probably to Mrs. Greer's benefit that she hadn't stuck around. "Luckily, the boy was smart enough to realize he had to keep people away from the shaft. His pa works in one of the mines, and he'd heard his pa talk about what could happen if a mine shaft were to collapse."

She shivered, knowing more could have been hurt. She was worried sick that Ben wouldn't come out of this alive, but she was thankful that no other child was in danger. It was a cold comfort, but a comfort, nonetheless.

She squeezed Jacob's hand. "Thank you for telling me. Where is the young man who kept Ben company and kept others from falling in?"

"Not sure. When the men arrived, his pa pulled him to the side, not wanting him to get hurt."

"Can you find him for me? I'd like to thank him for trying to help Ben." It was the least she could do. She was sure the boy was worried sick if he had been brave enough to stay behind.

"I can, but now doesn't seem right––"

"I need something to distract me, otherwise I might collapse into a heaping, inconsolable mess. I'm sure the boy needs reassurance that he did nothing wrong."

Jacob nodded and straightened to his full height. "All right. I'll see if I can find him, but first, I'm going to get you a bite to eat. I can't have you fainting dead away, and considering how quickly you disappeared after the morning meal, I'd venture to say you've had nothing today."

He was right, and her belly rumbled in response. While her head and heart didn't want to eat, she had to keep her strength up. It was going to be a long day waiting for word on her precious baby boy. She closed her eyes and clasped her hands to her chest as she prayed harder than she ever had that God would protect her son and those trying to rescue him.

Fifteen

The sun dropped behind the mountains, casting red and orange streaks across the dark blue sky. A multitude of lanterns were scattered around the mine shaft and across the open field. Cole's heart was heavy. They were no closer to getting Ben out of the mine shaft than they had hours before when he and Frannie arrived.

Her composure was hanging by a thread, but she did as she was asked and stayed out of the way. Jacob had pulled him aside and told him that Frannie had insisted on speaking with the young boys who had run for help and with the one who'd stayed behind. She'd wanted to make sure they were unharmed and thank them for getting help so quickly. Her thoughtfulness toward others was a testament to the caring woman she was.

They still didn't know if Ben had hurt himself or had fallen to his death. Either scenario was too horrible to contemplate, but Cole would prefer anything but death.

They had tried to slide a man through the mine shaft opening, but all the men were too broad in the shoulders. They needed someone smaller, with narrow hips and shoulders, and even then, they weren't sure it would work. Whoever they lowered inside had to be strong enough to hold the boy or have the wherewithal to secure him with a second set of ropes.

Jacob walked up to his side. A piece of straw hung from his mouth. He chewed on them when he was nervous, although no one would ever suspect he was. "Things aren't going well, are they?"

Cole rubbed the back of his neck and then stretched his arms above his head, his back cracking. "I'm afraid not. No one is small enough to go."

"What about digging around it?"

"I wish that was possible. The miners insist that the ground is too unstable."

"But you know mines. You and I both worked in 'em back East."

"I know that, and you know that, but we also don't know the terrain around here. The soil is different. I'm trusting those men who are familiar with the mine conditions here."

"What about sending a boy?" Jacob asked.

"We considered that, but none of them are strong enough to hold him. We fear that Ben'll be frightened if he's still awake and will fight whoever goes unless it's someone he knows."

"Then send me."

Cole whipped his head around and groaned. Frannie stood behind them with her hands on her hips, her face resolute. "Frannie, I don't——"

"I'm thinner than the men, and Ben knows me. He won't fight me, and I'm strong enough to hold him."

"It's not a good idea. He'll be frightened and out of sorts. If you can't get the rope around him, or slip, or any number of other things I don't even want to contemplate... Then we could lose you, too."

Her back straightened, her posture full of determination.

"Send me. I know you won't drop us. I can get a rope around him. He'll listen to me far better than anyone else."

"She has a point," Jacob said, rubbing his chin.

Cole glared at Jacob. "Maybe, but I can't lose you too, Frannie."

She pushed a finger hard into his chest. "And I can't lose our son. Tell those men you're going to lower me into the shaft. I'll need someone to get me a pair of boy's trousers. I can't wear my skirt and petticoats." She pushed her hair away from her face. "It's likely best I wear as little as possible so that I don't catch on anything. I'll tie my hair back and cover it with a kerchief." She took a breath. "Ben will do as I say. Once I get a second rope around his waist and under his arms, then he'll be secure if something were to happen. You'll be able to pull us both up."

"This is a lousy idea," Cole said, although a part of him thought her plan had merit. They had no other options save for sending one of the men's older boys, but even then, the same worry still stood. Ben would be much more likely to do as his mother bid than anyone else.

"Perhaps," Frannie said. "But it's clear we have no other options. I'd rather take the chance as opposed to a worse fate. You can either help me or I'll convince the men over there to do it." She pointed over her shoulder. "Either way, I'm going with or without your permission."

Frannie pulled the thin trousers over her hips. She had removed everything, including her corset, leaving her clad in only her chemise as she looked at the simple clothes laid out for her to wear. If Mrs. Greer caught sight of her, it would give her more ammunition to continue bad-mouthing her in town, but nothing mattered outside of saving her little boy. She couldn't fathom any other future without him and would be damned if she'd continue to sit by and do nothing. If this was her chance to do her part, then she would.

After ripping her chemise up and over her head, she took the long cloth and wrapped it around her chest, securing her breasts as tight as she could. She winced at the pain of binding them but better for them to be as flat as possible. She was kidding herself, though, if she could ever make her ample bosom smaller than it was, but she'd try her best.

The door behind her opened and shut. She grabbed a shirt off the bed and held it to her chest, muttering about people coming into rooms where they weren't welcome, when Cole's chuckle hit her ears.

"What are you doing here?" she said.

He held out his hands. "I'm sorry. I knocked, but you didn't answer. I wanted to make sure you were all right."

"As you can see, I'm fine, but I can't finish dressing with you standing there." She lifted an eyebrow as his gaze made a slow perusal of her trouser-clad form.

"Are you binding your breasts?" he asked.

"What kind of question is that?" A fiery blush ran up her chest and into her cheeks.

"One of many questions I need to ask to make sure you'll be as safe as I can make it while I drop the woman I love into a mine shaft where there's no telling what could happen."

She shook her head and hid her smile. She hated herself for smiling, but knowing he loved her filled her with comfort and resolve that she could do this. "Yes, I am binding them, so if you don't mind..."

He walked toward her and held out his hand. "Let me help."

"You shouldn't see me like this. It isn't proper." Not to mention the awareness of his presence made her skin tingle with anticipation.

"We're long past the point of being proper, my love. When

both you and Ben are safe in my arms, then we're going to make this official."

"What do you mean, make it official?" She hoped she knew what he was offering, but she wanted him to say it.

"Are you going to make me say it?" He quirked an eyebrow, a smirk on his lips.

"I believe there've been plenty of misunderstandings over the past few years. I don't think it's too much to ask of either of us to be precise," she said.

He took the shirt from her hands and dropped it on the bed. Turning her so her back was to him, he grabbed the cloth, and with careful thought and consideration, he straightened it and rewrapped it around her chest, his gaze burning into the back of her neck. His fingers were gentle, and his touch sent pinpricks of pleasure through her skin. Her mind needed to be on the task at hand, not on what those strong, gentle hands could do to her.

"I have every intention of you..." He paused, tucking the ends before resting his hands on her shoulders. His breath was hot and heavy against her ear. "Becoming my wife."

"Oh, really?" Her voice was wispy and low. She wasn't good at being coy, but she couldn't seem to help herself.

"Yes, really." He placed a soft kiss against her ear and pulled her back against him, holding her tight against his chest and resting his head against her neck. "I love you, Francesca Collins. I have from the moment I met you. My love started out as a friend and, over the years, blossomed into something more substantial that even I didn't recognize it for what it was. You and Ben are my everything. We *will* get him out of that mine shaft. Then I'm going to marry you proper in front of a preacher and God himself."

She sighed with contentment for the man she had always loved. Frannie turned, and his arms relaxed to let her face him. She raised her hands to his cheeks, cupping them between her fingers. His whiskers were rough against her palms. "I love you, too, Cole Seymour. I'd be honored to be your wife."

His lips dropped to hers in a sweet kiss that, while short and more like a quick peck, meant more than any searing kiss he had given her in the past. This kiss was the one they'd shared after declaring their feelings toward one another and held more meaning and love than anything before.

He dropped his forehead against hers. "If this were a different time, I'd have you naked and on that bed in a heartbeat."

She choked on a giggle. "And I'd let you."

His eyes twinkled at her impertinent remark.

"I love you, Cole."

His smile lit up the room. "I love you. Now"––he pulled back and rested his hands against her forearms––"let's get you dressed so we can save our son."

Twenty minutes later, they stood near the secure pulley. There was some grumbling among a few of the older men over the plan. The bolder young men who'd survived the war and who'd seen unspeakable things were more open-minded. They also realized the options to save the little boy were slim. Having her go into the shaft was the best possible course of action.

No one had heard a peep from Ben in hours, and they feared he was dead. No one said that to her; they were afraid she would lose her composure if they did. Cole held the harness for her as she lifted one leg into one hole and then the other. He slipped the harness up and over her hips and looped the ropes over her shoulders. He tightened the brace across her chest, his fingers steady as he checked to make sure it was secure.

Resting his hands on her shoulders, he said, "Does this feel all right? Is it too tight?"

She put her hands on his. "It feels good, and no, it's not too tight." She looked up at the pulley. "Will it be able to hold me?"

"Oh, yes, ma'am," the sheriff said, coming up alongside them. "This is as secure as could be. We have it anchored well away from the soft ground. You're as light as a feather, so it won't even notice the weight."

"Thank you," Cole said. "Are we ready?"

"Yes," he said. "But we want her to wear this to give her a bit of light." The sheriff lifted a canvas hat with a leather brim and metal lamp bracket attached to it. Once it was on her head, he struck a match and lit the candle. "Here is a packet of matches to stick in your trouser pocket. There's no guarantee the light will stay lit, but if you're careful and don't disturb the dirt too much, it should stay. Just in case, though, you'll have a packet to use if need be."

She took his hand between hers. "Thank you for everything, sheriff. I'll bake you a cake every week for the rest of your life when this is over."

He smiled. "No need for that, young lady. Let's get your son out of there. That'll be all the thanks I need."

He waved to the miners standing ready with the pulley and drew the metal carabiner toward her. Cole took it and secured it on the smaller carabiner resting against her back. It felt strange and heavy, but it gave her the support she needed.

Cole gazed at her. "Are you ready?"

"No," she said. "But I have to do this."

"You can change your mind. We can find another way."

She rested her hand on his arm. "There is no other way. You and I both know it." She took a deep breath to steady her nerves. "I'm ready."

Cole handed her the harness for Ben. She clutched it and then let him clip it to her chest so she wouldn't lose it when she was in the shaft. The ropes were tied together, so if she lost her grip, the pulley could bring them both up. She didn't understand how it worked, but the miners assured her they had things well in hand. Her job was to be as still as possible as they dropped her. She also had a whistle around her neck, tucked under her shirt, that she would use to blow when she found him.

Cole nodded. "She's ready."

The men cranked the pulley. She had to contain a small shriek when the pulley lifted her off the ground. Grasping the harness across her chest, she held on tight and prayed. A moment later, she swung over the deep, dark hole. The only light she would have was the stubby lamp on her head, and that paled in comparison to the darkness that would surround her. Taking a deep breath, she closed her eyes as they lowered her into the dark abyss.

Sixteen

Cole clenched his teeth as Frannie soared into the air before being lowered into the mine shaft. He wanted to yank her back into the safety of his arms, but he had to let her do this. The men were silent. The only ones moving were the ones operating the pulley. He'd been surprised by the sophisticated piece of machinery. He was familiar with them, having used them back East, but hadn't expected them to have one here.

Seeing it had given him a measure of peace, for the machinery would hold Frannie and Ben's weight with ease. What he feared more was the sides of the mine collapsing if she were to knock into the walls. It sounded as though it was an older mine shaft, although to say old was a misnomer. The mines in Virginia City hadn't been around for many years compared to the mines in Pennsylvania.

The miners weren't altogether too sure how stable the shaft was. It had been boarded over and ignored for years, but they were confident, or as confident as they could be, that Frannie had the best chance out of all of them. She was the only one small enough to fit. The fear on her face was mixed with rock-solid determination. Her love for Ben was the one thing keeping her from stopping the descent.

Her eyes were clamped shut, her fingers grasping the edge of the harness, but she held herself still, holding her elbows in and her knees tight together. She was following the miners' instructions to the letter, and he admired her bravery. He didn't know if he could do what she was doing. While he had worked in mines most of his life, he'd never been in tight quarters. As he got older, he'd spent less and less time inside them and more time inside the office dealing with the multitude of other issues related to the mine's operation.

Before he could blink, she disappeared from view. The only thing telling him she was still alive was the taut metal ropes extending out of the hole. The sound of the crank behind him should have relieved the fear, but with every turn, it dropped her farther and farther. The men had decided that the best course of action was to move slowly and steadily. They had no idea how far down Ben might be or if they had enough rope to reach him, although they were relatively convinced it wasn't far and she should find him.

Minutes ticked by. The lit lantern flickered as the wind picked up speed. They stopped for a few minutes when the gust grew. Hopefully, Frannie would remember what they had told her. If they stopped lowering her, it was only for her safety. She was not about to lose hope or worry. When the winds died, they would continue.

Finally, the crank started again, slowly and methodically.

Jacob came near his side and braced his hand against the back of Cole's shoulders. "How you holding up?"

Cole frowned. "As best as can be expected knowing I could lose both of them."

"You won't. She's strong and capable. Now that the two of you have reconciled, things can go right," Jacob said.

"She is. She's the bravest woman I know. I'm just sorry it took me so long to realize that."

Jacob's hand fell away. "I should have sent you that letter years ago, but I wrestled with the decision on whether I could betray her trust. When she revealed she was pregnant, she didn't tell me it was yours, but it didn't take much for me to figure out the truth."

"I don't blame you. I blame myself." Cole's guilt over what she had gone through made him desperate to correct the wrongs between them. "What made you decide to reach out now?"

"It was Ben who decided for me. I found him one afternoon a few months before I sent that letter. He was sitting in the hayloft, his face streaked with tears. Another one of the local boys had been teasing him about not having a pa. Somehow the boy had heard the rumor Mrs. Greer had been painting around town——that Ben was a bastard and that his ma was a whore."

Cole's skin crawled with irritation that anyone would dare call his Frannie a whore. She was as far from that as possible, but an unmarried woman, no matter the circumstances, often brought the gossipmongers out in full force, especially when the woman didn't have a family to support her.

"I'd sure like to box a few ears," Cole said.

Jacob laughed. "I felt the same, but trying to fight it with just words didn't seem prudent. There were already plenty of rumors that there was something nefarious going on between the two of us."

"Is there?" Cole immediately regretted he'd asked when he saw Jacob's face.

Jacob rubbed at his chin. "I suppose you have a right to ask that, but I thought you would've known me better than that." Jacob's voice was low but filled with something Cole couldn't identify. "I do love Frannie, as a sister. There has only been one man she has ever loved, and it ain't me. If she'd ever have looked at me the way she looks at you, I might've thought different, but she didn't, and she never will." Jacob reached into his back pocket, pulled out a piece of straw, held it in his hand, and looked at it even though the light was dim. Only the moon and the scattered lanterns gave off any light. "I'd do anything for her and Ben, which is why I sent that letter. Ben deserves his father, and Frannie deserves you. Don't disappoint me and give me cause to regret sending it."

Cole nodded, his throat tight at what Jacob had done for both him and Frannie.

"If you ever hurt her, I'll come back and skin you alive." Jacob laughed, but there was a sinister undertone that Cole would be wise to take to heart.

"I'll do my utmost to make her happy. I promise." That was a promise he would move heaven and earth to fulfill.

"You better." Jacob slapped him on the back. "Now, I need me a drink. This is gonna be a long night. Can I get you one?"

"No, thank you." He needed his wits about him while they waited.

Jacob ambled away, his shoulders sagging from the weight of the world or perhaps the weight of knowing he had tried to bring a family back together again and unforeseen circumstances might tear them apart instead.

Frannie's throat closed, and she struggled to get a good breath as the darkness and the tightness of the shaft wrapped around her. Over and over again, she repeated the words of the miner who'd instructed her on what to do. Keep your elbows in tight, lock your knees together, hold your head steady, straighten your feet, and don't move until or if you find Ben.

If you find Ben.

Those words haunted her. It wouldn't be if--it would be when. She couldn't lose hope, not if she could help it. As the pulley lowered her farther into the shaft, her skin burned from the tightness of the ropes. She'd have bruises and cuts when this was over, but it was a small price to pay if she could wrap her arms around Ben again.

She tried to focus on Cole's smiling face when he told her he loved her and the memories of Ben when he was born, when he took his first step, and when he called her momma for the first time. The happy thoughts were the only things that kept her from screaming and blowing the whistle in three short bursts to tell them she had to get out. She was to blow the whistle twice when she found Ben, three if she had to be removed immediately.

The shaft appeared to widen the farther down she went. She didn't know if that was a good thing, but every time she shifted, dirt dislodged from the sides. Wooden slats lined the walls. Most were intact, but a few had disintegrated from time and weather. The wood was likely the only thing keeping it from crumbling. Her feet hit a ledge, and it jarred her for a moment. As she scrambled to pull the whistle out from under her shirt, a soft whimper caught her attention.

"Ben," she called. "Ben, it's Momma. Is that you?"

A small cry, a few hiccups, and then the sweetest sound she had ever heard in all her years hit her ears.

"Momma." His voice was weak, but he was alive.

She tilted her head, trying to be careful of the walls, grateful the light on her lamp was still lit. It took her a moment, but then she saw him. He rested on a ledge, his small body curled into a ball. Somehow, he hadn't fallen any farther.

"Momma," he cried.

"Don't move, baby." She lowered her voice, trying to be soothing and calm, but she feared she sounded as scared as he felt. "Let me come to you. I don't want you to fall again."

She ripped out the whistle and held it, ready to blow it once she could touch him with her hands. It wouldn't do any good if she couldn't get to him. When he was within arm's reach, she puckered her lips and tried to blow, but her fingers trembled, and nothing emerged from the piece of metal between her lips. Taking a breath, she tried again and blew it once, twice. The sound echoed up the walls.

Ben cried and covered his ears, but it was a welcome sound. He was still alive, and that was all that mattered. Her descent into the shaft stopped, the ropes jarring. She put out her hand to stop the sudden swaying, and the walls held, although dirt and pebbles escaped from the seams between them and tumbled to the abyss below.

She grasped the harness they'd given her for Ben and reached for him. He tried to stand, but he held his arm near his chest, the angle of it wrong, and cried when he moved it.

"I'm so sorry, baby. This is going to hurt, but we have to get you out of here. Can you help Momma?"

He sniffled but nodded. She made quick work of strapping him into it, trying to be mindful of his broken arm, but unfortunately nudged it one too many times. Ben's tears were almost her undoing. He tried to be strong, but suffering lined his sweet face. Soon, she had him nestled in her arms and kissed his weary cheeks.

"Close your eyes for me, Ben. It's going to be dirty going up, and I don't want the dust to get in your eyes."

"Am I going to fall, Momma?"

The fear in his voice made her want to protect him as best she could. She had to be strong for him.

"No," she said. "The miners are going to pull us up. You just need to hold as still as possible, keep your face near my shirt, close your mouth, and try to breathe through your nose."

He nodded. She lifted the whistle and blew it once. The shrill sound made Ben whimper, but he did as she asked and stayed quiet in her arms. A moment later, the ropes pulled tight and dragged her and Ben up the shaft.

Dirt shifted and fell as the space between her and the walls shrunk with Ben's added girth, but she kept her arms solidly around his waist as he buried his face into her shoulder, doing as she bid. She was so proud of his bravery, and she whispered as such to him as they moved. Her skin was bruised and raw, but when her head emerged from the dark, dank hole, she breathed in the fresh air. She had never been so grateful to see the night sky.

When she and Ben were out of the shaft, cheers of joy rang out around them. Ben startled in her arms and raised his head.

"What's that, Momma?" His dirt-streaked face was a precious gift she would never take for granted again.

"That," she said, "is the merry sound of everyone being glad we're alive and out of that hole."

The pulley swung them to steady ground, and Cole's firm hands gripped her waist until her feet were firmly on the ground. Her nerves were strung thin, the worry over what could have happened rushing through her, causing her to stumble, but Cole held her secure, stalwart and strong next to her.

Jacob stepped close and lifted Ben away. Ben's cries of pain filled the air.

"Please be careful. I think his arm's broken," Frannie said. "I don't know if he has any other injuries. I couldn't tell. There wasn't enough light for me to see. I just wanted to get him out of there."

"You did right by getting him out of there quick, Fran. The doc'll look him over," Jacob said.

Jacob knelt, placing Ben on the ground. Miners had brought more lanterns to their side, and the town doctor rushed over. They laid Ben on a stretcher, and the doctor gave him a quick going-over.

"His arm is broken, but that looks like the extent of any major injuries. Let's get him back to my surgery, where I can look him over more closely. I think he'll be fine." He smiled at Frannie and squeezed her hand. "You did well, my dear." Looking at Cole, he said, "Bring her with you to the surgery. I want to look her over too. Make sure she doesn't have any scrapes or cuts that need tending to."

Jacob and another man picked up the stretcher and followed the doctor.

"Jacob," she called. "Watch over him, please. I'll be there as soon as they untie me from this contraption."

"You know I will, Fran. He won't be out of my sight, I promise."

Relief rushed through her. Jacob would watch over him while Cole tended to her.

Men walked by, shook her hand, touched her shoulder, and uttered words of gratitude and awe at her bravery. Most of the men knew how dangerous it'd been for her to go into that shaft. Between the tight quarters and the chance that, with one wrong move, she could have collapsed the whole shaft––they were impressed. It'd be a story that many would talk about for years to come.

When the last of the men had left and the lights from the lanterns all but disappeared except for the one near their feet, Cole finally released her from the ropes and carabiners securing her to the pulley. His touch was gentle, caring, but his fingers trembled.

She placed her hands over his and stopped him. "Cole, are you all right?"

"Am I all right?" he said, shuddering. "I'm more than all right, but I could've lost you both."

"But you didn't," she murmured. "We did it. We saved our son."

"No." He shook his head so fast his brown hair fell across his forehead. "*You* saved our son."

"I couldn't have done it without you. You gave me the strength to do it. Ben needs his mother and his father. We need to tell him tonight that he has a father, and I couldn't be prouder to call you that."

Cole looked into her eyes, grazing his thumbs against her dirty cheeks. "I love you so much, Francesca Marie. You gonna keep that promise and still be my wife?"

"Only if you promise to put up with my stubborn nature, my insolent attitude, and my undying love for you."

"That sounds like a promise that'll be easy to keep."

He bent his head and placed his lips against hers. The sky exploded in a vibrancy of pinks, purples, and blues as the sun rose. It was a new day, a new beginning, and one they would never ever take for granted again.

Epilogue

August 15, 1881

Cole shook the reins, and the four workhorses strapped in front of the freight wagon groaned under the weight of the stacked pine tree logs. His two oldest sons, Ben and Stanley, sat next to him, their faces brimming with excitement. They had moved to the ranch that rested an hour outside of Helena seven years ago, and after much trial and error, they were making progress. The cattle were thriving, and they were finally finishing up the porch of the new ranch house he had promised Frannie when they moved there.

They had left Virginia City right after Stanley was born in 1871, when the gold mines ran dry. The boarding house had dwindled in boarders, and it'd become almost impossible for them to make a decent living. Deciding to leave, they'd headed North, where Cole struck it rich in a strange set of circumstances in a place called Confederate Gulch. There had been a gold rush in the late 1860s, and many believed the gold had run dry. On a whim, Cole had bought an abandoned claim, and after six months of pure luck and hard work, he'd struck it rich, getting more gold than they could ever spend in a lifetime.

After he got what he could off the claim, they'd left for Helena, and a few months later, they'd found the ranch. It contained a small two-bedroom house with a loft and a few head of cattle that the prior owner was in a hurry to sell. Her husband had passed away unexpectedly, and she'd been moving back East to be near her family. She'd been thrilled with the offer Frannie and Cole had made, and they had moved into the ranch house with their three children, Ben, Stanley, and Luke. After a bit of trial and error, Cole had learned the ins and outs of ranching pretty quickly, but as their family grew, so did the need for a new home.

Jacob had left Virginia City after they rescued Ben from the mine shaft. Once satisfied Ben would be all right, he had finally left to do his exploring, achieving the dream he had sought since he was a little boy. They'd seen little of him over the years, but on occasion, he would stop by for a night or two, telling the boys of his adventures. He had even struck up a special relationship with Cole's second son, Stanley, calling him his little buck. Jacob still held a special place in his heart for Ben, but something about Stanley reached out to him. Whenever Jacob visited, he and Stanley would go out and rough it for a few nights, always coming home covered in dirt, mud, and who knew what else, but always with a happy smile and a contentment that all was right with the world.

"Pa," Ben said, "Are we going to build an arch?"

Cole smiled, massaging the leather reins under his fingertips. "Yes, son, we are."

"Why?" Stanley asked, his voice high-pitched and exuberant.

"Because your ma thought we needed to let folks know where they are."

"Wouldn't they know that already?" Stanley asked. "We've lived here forever, so everyone around these parts knows us."

"Don't be stupid, Stanley," Ben said.

"Benjamin, don't call your brother stupid."

"Yes, sir," he mumbled.

Out of the corner of his eye, Cole saw Stanley stick his tongue out at his brother. Ben's face was red with irritation, but he swallowed it back and tried to ignore his younger brother. Ben tried to be patient with his brothers but struggled, being the eldest of six.

Cole still couldn't believe that he and Frannie had that many children. They hadn't planned on it, but God had other ideas. After Ben, they were blessed with Stanley, Luke, Michael, and then his two precious girls, Anne and Katie. All of them were a handful but each a joy in their own way. He wasn't altogether sure they wouldn't have more, but Frannie insisted she was done and gave him a look that he'd regret it if he dared to impregnate her again. But he knew that if they were blessed with more, she would be just as wonderful to them as she was to their other six.

Cole pulled on the reins to slow the horses to a stop. He shoved the brake with his foot to lock it into place, looped the reins around the brake handle, and turned to look at his two boys. "We're here."

"Yay!" Stanley jumped over the side of the wagon, his enthusiasm contagious.

Ben followed at a more sedate pace, trying to act more like an adult than his fourteen years granted him. He was trying to spread his wings and had the scars to show it. The two of them had had a few rows recently, but he was a good boy trying to step into the shoes of a man.

Cole thanked God every day that Ben had survived that harrowing mine shaft experience. He'd had a broken arm but had recovered as quickly as children often do. He rarely brought it up. Cole and Frannie weren't too sure he remembered it and wanted to keep it that way. It still made Cole's heart stick in his throat to think of how he could have lost both of them that day, but thankfully, he hadn't.

Cole climbed down, his body not as spry as it had been, but

still could move like the best of them. He reached into the back of the wagon and pulled out the feed bags for the horses, handing two to Ben. Looping one over a horse's head, he rubbed the space between his ears, and the horse nudged him but dug into the feed. He finished with the other and then walked to the back of the wagon.

"Boys," he said, "come here."

Ben finished feeding the other two horses and followed Stanley to Cole's side. Looping an arm over each of their shoulders, Cole turned so they were facing the mountains at the far edge of the ranch. He knelt to be near Stanley's level. "Now, Stanley, you wanted to know why your ma wanted us to put up the arches?"

"Yes, Pa." Stanley slapped a mosquito on his arm.

"Well, your ma, being the fine woman she is––"

"Yes, she is," Stanley hollered. "She's the best Ma in the whole wide world."

"Stop it, you knucklehead," Ben said. "Quit trying to butter up Pa. He knows how special Ma is."

"Now, Ben. Don't be harsh to your brother or be calling him names. You're to lead by example, and saying such things ain't kind nor tolerated. You know better."

"Yes, Pa." Ben's voice was contrite. "Sorry, I'll do better."

"I know you will," Cole said. "Now, as I was saying. Your ma deserves so much. I wanted to make this the best home in the world for her. She took one look at the mountains over yonder." He pointed to the vast mountain range in the distance, the peaks rising out through the fluffy white clouds. "And decided that we needed to call our home Thundering Mountain Ranch."

"Why?" Ben asked. "Thundering sounds strange. Mountains don't thunder."

"That's true, Ben." He paused as his memories floated back to that day they had stopped at the property line of the ranch. "You boys don't remember this, but when we arrived, it was thundering and lightning something fierce. We huddled under the wagon, waiting for the storm to subside, watching the lightning burst from the sky, slapping the ground and shaking everything around us."

"I remember that," Ben said.

"So do I," Stanley said. "It was really scary."

"You don't remember that. You were only a baby." Ben scowled.

"I do too," Stanley said, scrunching his face in frustration. "It was raining and—"

"And nothing. You're only saying that 'cause Pa said it."

"Ben, that's enough. Remember what I said."

"Yes, Pa," Ben muttered, his angst at being reprimanded once again sticking in his craw, and while Ben knew better than to push his luck, he'd been a trial to both Cole and Frannie lately. Cole was sure Ben would grow out of it once he flexed his muscles and grew into the fine man he was sure to become.

"As I was saying." Cole tried to keep his patience with the constant interruptions, but he couldn't complain. His children were a handful at the best of times, but he wouldn't change a thing about any of them. He had everything he never thought he'd wanted, and it made his heart soar knowing he'd been lucky in finding it. "When we arrived, it was thundering like crazy. Your ma looked out from under the wagon and watched the lightning strikes near the mountain range and knew within a few minutes that the best name for our new home would be Thundering Mountain Ranch."

"But why does she want us to make an arch?" Stanley asked, tugging on his ear.

"Because she wants everyone to know that our place is called Thundering Mountain, and she says it's only proper that the arch says as such."

"That don't make sense," Stanley mumbled. "We've lived here forever, and no one has ever wondered what the name of the ranch was called."

Cole laughed. "I suppose it doesn't, but it's what your ma wants, so it's what we're going to give her, all right?"

"Yes, Pa," Stanley said, fidgeting in his desire to get started.

"Yes, Pa," Ben said.

"All right then. Let's get started, shall we?" He pushed to stand and saw the love of his life sauntering down the dirt road, holding their youngest daughter, Katie, in her arms.

"Boys, your ma is coming."

"Ma!" Stanley scampered toward Frannie and stopped when he reached her side. She ruffled his hair with her fingers. The love on her face clear.

Stanley took her hand in his and pulled her to Cole's side.

"Hey, darling." Cole kissed her on the cheek and took Katie, tickling her under the chin and making her squirm with delight.

Stanley pulled Frannie toward the wagon, chattering a mile a minute about what they were doing. Her smile was radiant as she listened to both Ben and Stanley as they told her about their morning. They were each determined to show their ma what they had done.

Cole looked at them, his heart full. He couldn't ask for more. He had a beautiful, vivacious wife who carried all six of his children without complaint, cared for them like no other, supported him in the decision to move to this little place of heaven, and loved him every night as though it was their first time.

∼

Thank you for reading *Beneath the Thundering Sky*. I hope you enjoyed catching a glimpse of how Cole and Frannie got their happily ever after.

The **Thundering Mountain Ranch** series continues in book two with Ben and Elizabeth's story *Thundering Mountain* where Ben's hunt for a traditional wife ends with an untraditional wife instead.

The third book in the series *Thundering Meadows* is where Elizabeth's brother, James, finds love on a derailed train with a woman who delivers her second baby straight into his arms. James offers Rose a marriage of convenience that will test their loyalty and trust with one another.

The fourth book in the series *Thundering Ridge* is Luke and Louisa's story taking place in the heart of Helena, Montana. An evil parlor house madam tries to sell Louisa to the highest bidder and continues to further wreak havoc on Luke's family. Luke and Louisa will have to navigate wickedness at every turn to finally get their happily ever after.

The fifth book in the series *Thundering Snow* is Stanley and Charlotte's story. It begins when Charlotte falls straight into Stanley's lap during a barroom brawl. He agrees to help search for her father and it is a race to find someone who does not want to be found.

Note: *Thundering Snow* is on preorder and will be released soon.

If you'd like to know when my next book will be released you can sign up for my mailing list on my website - nicoleneiswanger.com or follow me on Twitter, Facebook, Instagram, or Threads.

About the Author

Nicole is a Senior Business Analyst by day, a reader during meal time, and a writer while watching historical dramas. She discovered her passion for writing during a summer vacation when her husband's truck died. While being stranded for five days with nothing to occupy her time she began writing. She writes historical American West romances set in the heart of Montana with swoonworthy cowboys and feisty, independent women. She holds an MFA from Southern New Hampshire University, an MS from Strayer University, and BA from St. Leo University.

Please reach out via her website www.nicoleneiswanger.com or directly at nicole@nicoleneiswanger.com.

Help other readers find this book by writing a review with your favorite retailer or by sharing on your favorite social media platform.

 facebook.com/nicoleneiswanger.author
 x.com/NNeiswanger1
instagram.com/nneiswangerauthor

Also by Nicole Neiswanger

Made in United States
Troutdale, OR
11/25/2024

25259449R00092